The Forgotten Sister

EMMA HARDWICK

Drina
ROMANCE
PUBLISHING

COPYRIGHT

Title: The Forgotten Sister

First published in 2022

Copyright © 2022

CONTENTS

1

DORSET STREET

"Joey Cornish! Get down from there this instant! Do you hear me—you little—!"

The beleaguered mother craned her head towards the dark Whitechapel sky, her eyes locked onto a silhouetted pair of ragged feet poking over the roof tiles.

She wasn't the only one struggling to find the right word to define the lad. You couldn't use *'hooligan,'* as it insinuated a lusty lack of self-control. *'Scoundrel'* implied that he was crooked and untrustworthy. *'Villain'* didn't work because it smacked of evil criminality, and *'rogue'* was far too mature and conniving. The only word that came close to describing Joey Cornish was *'rascal,'* which was more closely related to mischief than menace.

"Down, lad! Now! Or so help me—"

The weather was fine. The permanent resident, a shroud of smoke and mist that hung over the East End, had dispersed for a short while. A fresh wind was dawdling south, and Joey could hardly smell the foul Thames. There was seldom a hiatus in the gloom of the East End, but tonight the moonbeams lit the alleys way better than the yellow gas lamps ever could. Instead of nature creating an uplifting experience, it exposed the exhausted desperation of Dorset Street.

Joey sat on the roof's parapet, swinging his legs as they dangled over the broken gutter. The tenement block he lived in had four storeys, and the higher it rose, the more the structure leaned over the street. The building had never been designed to look that way. The poorly built walls had deteriorated quickly and evolved into an impressive facsimile of a medieval structure. It was as if they were trying to shield the street below.

If Joey had leaned forward just a tad, he would have hurtled down to the filthy cobbles beneath. The mildew on the slate roof was slippery and treacherous. There were large holes between some of the tiles that exposed the rafters. When Joey looked down, he had a bird's eye view of the stairwell. It became narrower as it descended to the ground floor. When Joey bent forward to take a closer look, the deceitful dirty steps sometimes beckoned him to jump.

He looked over the rooftops and the great chimneys of London. They stretched far into the distance. He'd forgotten how big the city was. His circumstances didn't often allow for romantic ideas, but Joey decided he would dream a little. What harm could dreams do? It would be sacrilege if he allowed a night of clear skies and breathtaking stars to escape a thorough observation. Joey lay back on the tiles and stared at the magnificent heavens.

Peace was a rare commodity in Dorset Street. The lad could hear the loud drunken festivities of the people down below, distracting him and puncturing his quiet solitude. He'd no opportunity to relish the beauty of the moment. Joey hated Saturday nights.

From a young age, he had sought refuge on the rooftop. There, he escaped his mother's abusive male friends and the local bully boys. It was a place where he could find peace. In the winter, he would sit between the chimneys. He found more warmth huddled next to the clay pots than in the room he shared with his mother. Joey would only climb down from the roof when the sun arose, and there was a brief lull in the madness.

Joey watched the people below him as they caroused and stood around open fires. The prostitutes' horrid shrieks mingled with the falsetto of a fiddle. The grating of wire against wire wouldn't die until someone in the street did. Men took the opportunity to grope any woman who would allow it, grabbing at their bosoms, lifting their dresses, and worse. The whores would take them as close as they could to ecstasy and then stand back and make their price. They all demanded payment up front, and their knickers didn't come off until the silver crossed their palm. Some women had rooms where they provided their services. Others simply went off into an alleyway. Around Whitechapel, it wasn't unheard of to take the man back to your husband's house—with him still in it.

Joey knew them all. Lucy Crawford was old, so she couldn't afford a room and paid to use her friend's bed. Anna Miller took men back to her father's flat, and her father managed the financial side of the transaction. Bunty Jones had a room in Miller's court. It was hardly the size of a birdcage and just as dirty. Joey and his mother lived in one room, and while she did business, Joey had to be gone. Desperate, old and used women accepted pennies because they had lost their looks. The younger girls were competitive, and they fought amongst each other like cats.

The pimps were brutal men. They would negotiate time, place, price, discounts, and services. Some allowed the punters to test the merchandise for free. Ruthless, they punished the prostitutes and 'Johns' alike. Nelly Evans had her face beaten in repeatedly. Finally, Big Eric had murdered her and a customer as they tried to flee from him. One thousand people watched when Big Eric was executed. Most of the audience had never known him, but they cheered as his legs stopped jittering and his body went slack. This didn't bring Nelly back from the dead, and there were plenty more 'Big Erics' where that one came from.

The street had two doctors. The short fat one, Dr Green, was from Manchester, an overly jovial little fellow. Rumour had it that he was happy to forgo payment and trade in carnal pleasures or bottles of ale. Poor people always had more beer than money. Joey had once looked at his hands, and his fingers resembled fat porkers, and he always had a fag dangling between his plump lips. The other one, Dr Pratt, had a very posh accent. He didn't live in Dorset Street, but he had a surgery on the second floor of number three. Someone had mentioned that he was from Harley Street. Dr Pratt had been stripped of his medical licence for helping women drop their foetuses. Joey didn't understand what any of this meant until his mother told him in no uncertain terms.

"He rips 'em bairns from their bellies. Then he takes what's left to the privy and dumps it there."

Joey had found the explanation so revolting that he'd refused to use the privy for a week, choosing to squat on the pavement after dark. There was so much horse muck in the street that they would never notice his contribution.

The landlords had the most power, and everyone was afraid of them. Joey recalled the night Mr Gamble had evicted Ma Moody. The Moody's were an Irish family of fourteen, and they all lived in one room. Mr Gamble had evicted them in the dead of winter. Ma Moody had frozen to death while she held her grandchild. The baby fell out of the dead woman's arms and lay on the pavement until it also died.

Mr Lune never came out of his room, and nobody ever bothered him. Joey always thought Mr Lune was a timid man until he heard Bill Turner tell Wally Anderson that Mr Lune was the wealthiest man in the East End.

"How so?" chuckled Wally.

"Counterfeit notes," was all Billy said.

Joey asked a few people what 'counterfeit' meant, but nobody knew. Eventually, he asked Billy himself. Billy hit him about the ears.

"Where did you hear that?" Billy hissed into Joey's deaf ear.

Joey was terrified and hoped the truth would set him free.

"I heard you talking to Wally about Mr Lune," Joey confessed.

Billy's face turned scarlet. He struck Joey again. Henceforth, Joey was much more cautious about his lines of questioning. It took months to learn what 'counterfeit' meant, and by that time, old Mr Lune was dead.

Joey didn't know what happened to Mr Lune's money when the old man died, but there were many people in and out of his house all night long. The only person who came out with something odd-looking was Billy Turner. He carried a hatbox. It was a rather feminine accessory for a man of his brutish stature. Billy was straining under the weight of whatever was inside it.

At the end of a street was a door set into a wall. A grown man would have to bend to go through it. It was the scariest place in Dorset Street... No, it was the second scariest place. The first was that room in Miller's Court where Miss Kelly was murdered. Joey never went near it. An alleyway led into Miller's Court, and Joey refused to look down it. He got the shivers and felt compelled to run. Joey wasn't even born when Paul the Ripper prowled the streets. He'd heard the story hundreds of times, and every time it became worse. Only as an adult would Joey realise that his mother had not exaggerated the horror. The old people would sit around and discuss how Miss Kelly was mutilated. They would take out the bits and bobs they had stolen from her room as souvenirs. Nobody believed that the coppers had caught the real Ripper.

The little door that was set into the wall led to where the Broadhurst brothers lived. They were five blokes who had grown up on the street, and legend had it that they had always been bad. Nobody ever saw them, but Joey's mother had repeated the urban legend of how the Broadhurst brothers had ripped out someone's tongue. Joey always crossed the road when he reached that end of the street. He didn't want to be seen anywhere near that door. Little did anyone know that the Broadhurst family were good sorts and that it was Mr Broadhurst, the patriarch, who had committed a vile murder. His wife and sons had lost everything and were too ashamed to be seen publicly. But the legend was driven into the hearts and souls of every child on the street.

Like in every bad place, there were also good people. Joey knew who he could approach for a crust of bread. The Irish were squashed into close quarters, but if Joey's mother put him out of the house for a night, the Mulroney family would take him in.

The locals thought the Jews were curious folk. They never spoke to anyone. The men had long beards, and they all dressed strangely with funny caps. Their children were well cared for, but they were not allowed to play with Joey. They were nowhere to be seen on Saturdays. They all disappeared. Joey knew if he was hungry, Mrs Herzl would feed him. Mrs Herzl never smiled. She would push the food through the door and close it quickly. Joey was terrified of her.

Joey didn't indulge in self-pity. This was his life, and he'd experienced no other. He had a good sense of humour, and there was a lot to be happy about. Joey understood people. Although he couldn't read a book, he could read a face. He'd not been taught arithmetic, but Joey could add and subtract pounds, shillings, and pence. He understood card games, horse races and fafi. He used the sirens at the factories to tell the time.

Joey looked at the street below him. Joey made a decision. He wouldn't live in Dorset Street forever. Nor would he live in Whitechapel, Spitalfields, Wapping, or any of London's East End.

The fate that Joey had been born into was not to be his destiny. His life was about to change forever—even more than if he fell off the high roof. He just didn't know how yet.

2

THE DISAPPOINTING DAUGHTER

Clarice Lawrence felt her temper rise the instant she stepped into her mother's ostentatious home.

It was a miserable Saturday afternoon in London, and she'd walked from Chelsea to Kensington in the howling wind. Clarice was disgusted that her mother, name Martha Lawrence, had stooped so low as to send her a note demanding her company under the auspices of being deathly ill.

The young woman looked around her, taking in the scene. The house was teeming with guests, primarily politicians, a few music hall impresarios and artistes, and a slew of fading aristocratic sorts.

Martha saw her daughter and made a beeline towards her.

"Clarice," she cooed, making a show in front of her guests.

Everyone turned around to look at the newcomer. Nobody knew much about Clarice Lawrence, and she liked it that way. The only thing they knew for a fact was that she was beautiful but had an appalling dress sense.

"Oh, hello, my dear," Martha greeted, looking down her nose at Clarice.

"Is my father here?" asked Clarice, glancing about the room.

Martha ignored the question. She and her husband had separate lives, thank goodness.

"Thank you for coming, my darling," Martha said, continuing her act.

"Your note said you were very ill," hissed Clarice.

"I felt so much better a few days ago that I decided to have a few friends over to celebrate my good health," said Martha, wiping her forehead with the back of her hand for dramatic effect.

"They must have been desperate for a free meal if they accepted an invitation at such short notice," Clarice snapped, annoyed by the blatant lie.

Martha could have slapped her daughter for the comment and would have if they had been alone.

"You lied to me, Mama," Clarice accused her coolly.

"Don't refer to me as 'Mama' in public. Call me 'mother', or nothing at all. 'Mama' is common and provincial."

"We are common and provincial, Mama. You are a minor industrialist's daughter, and my father's family were farmers."

"Landed gentry, my dear, keep to my facts when you are in public," Martha Lawrence instructed her daughter.

"And please introduce yourself as Clarice. Nicknames infer that we are familiar with each other."

"No fear of overt affection, Mama. God forbid there is any display of intimacy between mother and daughter."

"Don't you dare blaspheme in this house, Clarice," Martha scolded, but her daughter had already turned her back and was walking away.

*

Martha Lawrence had a frenzied social calendar. There was bridge, charity benefits, tea parties and mountains of other activities, which the bored invented to entertain each other. Usually, women attended these events, but on Saturday afternoons, Martha would invite entire families to afternoon tea. On Sunday mornings, she was always at the end of the ninth pew at

St Joseph's Parish Church, where the great and the good atoned for their sins. It was the only seat that she could afford.

Dame Martha Lawrence loved entertaining. It enabled her to show off her beautiful home, eat as much cake as she could stuff into her already round body, and fish for new gossip. Clarice's father, Frank Lawrence, had recently remarked that his wife was beginning to take on the shape of a teapot, and the amount of jam that stuck to her mouth made her look like a glazed cherry. Neither observation was flattering.

*

Martha had worked hard and showed great fortitude on the long, lonely road to social recognition. Her tenacity was commendable as she navigated the peaks and troughs of elitism.

She realised that most of the aristocracy were broke. They were willing to take anything they could get for free. Nothing gave the gentry more satisfaction than wafting their wealth under the noses of the aristocracy, who retaliated by reciting their detailed pedigree. They found it empowering to communicate that they were five hundredth in line to the throne.

After exploiting the politics of the classes, Martha finally succeeded in her quest to be included. If the invitations on her mantle shelf were anything to go by, she'd succeeded in becoming an integral cog in the great wheel of English culture.

Frank Lawrence was a wealthy man who had become rich in the American gold rush. He'd taken his winnings, as he called his profit, and returned to England. Once home, he'd purchased a shabby piece of land from an even more shabby Duke. The duke was stone broke and overjoyed to have a little income. This caused a Royal furore, and Frank Lawrence sold the property back to the crown, making a considerable profit. The Royals incentivised Frank to keep schtum about the affair by giving him a Knighthood.

Twenty-five-year-old Clarice abhorred her mother's forceful personality. Behind Martha's deferential public image lay a monster. Alone with her family, without anyone to impress, Martha Lawrence was a domineering bully. Frank Lawrence chose to avoid his wife to the extent that he purchased a townhouse for her in London. It was here that Clarice found herself trapped in a sea of pompous socialites. Clarice didn't care what anybody thought of her. She loved her freedom. Martha had tried to enforce her will upon Clarice. By the age of eighteen, Clarice felt like a wild animal that would die in captivity.

Frank had inspired Clarice to leave home and forge a life of her own. Clarice had gone to her father's home years before, delighted to escape the gilded cage she'd lived in. Frank knew what it was like to be young and crave adventure. Clarice, his daughter, was just like him.

Frank didn't love or like his wife at all. He would have bought her a house in New York and Paris if it guaranteed he would never see her again. For the moment, the place in London sufficed.

Frank could remember his wife's response to his decision as if it were yesterday. She had been livid.

"We have to discuss Clarice's future," Martha snapped.

"What is there to discuss?"

"She needs some refinement to find a suitable husband."

"What is wrong with her?" Frank demanded.

"She is a stupid girl who has ridiculous ideas in her head."

Martha was jealous of Frank's love for his daughter.

"No, she isn't," Frank argued.

"She is reading strange books about history. I find her painting and drawing when she should be attending social functions. Her poetry books are all over the place, and she dresses like a peasant."

"This isn't the dark ages, Martha. It's—bohemian."

"I don't care," Martha said in an assertive tone. "I demand that you enrol her in a Swiss finishing school where she can be taught social etiquette and be turned into an acceptable human being."

Frank lost his temper.

"How dare you say these things about my daughter? Listen to yourself. You should be ashamed. There is nothing wrong with Clarice, and I am not paying for a Swiss Finishing School."

"You will do what I tell you to," snapped Martha.

"No, Martha, I will not. Clarice wants to attend London University, and I have enrolled her in her chosen course."

Martha was shocked.

"You made this decision without consulting me?" Martha asked coldly.

"She will study Ancient History and Egyptology."

"Such fine subjects for a young woman and homemaker. They will serve her well."

"Stop being ridiculous, woman. I also gave her permission to choose where she wants to live. If she stays with you, you will make her life a living hell."

Frank had never been as serious as this day, and his last words were ruthless.

"If you don't obey my wishes or create any discord, I will sell the house in London, and you can come back to the country and live as the farmer's wife that you are."

Martha was wise and held her tongue. Inside she seethed with hatred for the common man that she'd married.

Clarice had not lived with her shrew of a mother for years and seldom saw her. So, it was almost the end of the world for Martha when Clarice chose to live in Chelsea.

"I have not raised you to live in a place with people like that," Martha said.

"I like where I live, mother. The rent is cheap, the wine is cheaper, and I am surrounded by like-minded people—unlike here."

"You are an embarrassment. How can you do this to me, after everything I have given you. Is this how you repay me?"

*

Clarice's small bolthole in Chelsea was her refuge. She'd chosen it for the large windows and French door that led onto a small balcony. The rooms were on the third floor of a tired old townhouse, which had once been fabulous. The staircase to the third floor was rickety and something of a death trap due to a few planks missing here and there. Every passer-by walking along the corridor could be heard as clear as a bell, with the floor creaking rhythmically below their heels.

Clarice and her father, Frank, enjoyed a close relationship. As distant as she was with Martha, the opposite pertained to her father. They would often meet for coffee or meals. Frank loved discussing Clarice's studies and monitoring her sure progress.

After Clarice had moved into her apartment, she invited her father to tea. She was proud of her small home. Frank was intrigued and impressed by Clarice's eclectic taste. He often found himself distracted by her unusual collections.

The apartment was scattered with a conglomeration of books, paintings, and artefacts arranged in no particular order. The furniture was layered with ethnic blankets made with mohair from Turkey and camel hair from the middle east. She'd chosen bright wallpaper in solid colours, and large crystal chandeliers hung from the moulded ceilings. The apartment had no particular style, and the furniture didn't match. She had a large, purple buttoned sofa placed on a red, black, and mustard Afghan rug.

Clarice would serve tea on an Arabian tea table. The teapot was Royal Dalton chintz or earthenware from Japan. The mismatched cups and saucers showed her impatience with searching for the correct, *'expected'* combinations. Although the presentation was chaotic, the crockery was beautiful.

Clarice had two ornate French chairs painted snow-white and upholstered in the brightest yellow Chinese silk. There were carpets upon carpets. Tablecloths upon tablecloths. Her home was warm, layered, and interesting. Frank didn't want to see her bedroom. He was plagued with every father's nightmare that he may find a clue suggesting that his daughter had a *'gentleman-friend.'*

*

At the party, Clarice felt claustrophobic between the bustles and the thick smell of rosewater. She needed to make her way to a more private part of the house to avoid the gossipy throng. The door gently closed as she left the room and slipped into the library.

The library was bathed with golden light, a dying fire burning behind the grate. The dark atmosphere was soothing, and she was relieved to be alone and in peace. She moved towards the drinks cabinet and poured herself a glass of sherry. She flopped into an oversized leather chair next to the fire and took a sip of the sweet, comforting liquid.

"I knew it wouldn't take long for a like-minded sort to join me."

The voice was young, fresh, and educated. She looked across the dusty room and saw the voice's owner lounging on a sofa.

Clarice stared at the fellow, annoyed that he'd not made himself known earlier.

"It's Thomas McGill," the man announced, displaying all the confidence in the world.

"Do you mind if I take the seat opposite you?" Thomas asked good-naturedly, sitting down well before he was given permission. "We will be able to see each other, and I won't feel like a voyeur."

The comment was meant to make him sound enigmatic, but it failed. The pitch of his voice was too high to belong to a more dashing man.

"May I pour you something to drink?" Clarice asked him.

He nodded, and she poured more of the deep reddish-brown liquid into a crystal glass. Clarice handed it to McGill. He deliberately brushed his hand against hers as he took it. Clarice pulled her hand away roughly and wiped it on her skirt.

"It is lovely to see you again, Miss Lawrence," he said, turning on the charm.

"Have we met before?" Clarice asked.

Thomas seemed taken aback. Women didn't usually forget him.

"Yes, we met at the charity ball that my mother held for the Crown Street Orphanage."

"You are mistaken," said Clarice. "I am never invited to charity balls."

"Then, I am wrong," Thomas apologised, feeling stupid.

Clarice had heard a lot about the man in front of her. He was in his mid-twenties and the spoilt, only son of Lord and Lady McGill, who owned a considerable amount of land in Wales. Their only competition in that area was the Duke himself, who only outclassed them by a few hectares and the title HRH. The McGill family made regular pilgrimages to London. The country was far too dull for their taste. While in London, young Thomas ensured he exploited everything the city had to offer. He frequented every theatre and nightclub that had sprung up almost overnight. It was unusual to see him during daylight hours. Clarice guessed he'd squirrelled himself away in the dark library to recover from a boozy night on the town. His father, Lord McGill, couldn't keep himself away from the clubs of Pall Mall or the more nefarious side of Soho. With her husband mostly absent, Lady McGill was desperate to find a lover. Alas, even the types of bounders who made a sport out of bedding married women had avoided her.

Thomas McGill's short, dark brown hair was pasted flat against his head in accordance with the latest style. His knees were crossed in the relaxed manner of one pretending to be nonchalant and superior. His eyes were pitch black in his snow-white face, which made him resemble a bull terrier. He had no hair on his face, the skin looked soft, and his hands were professionally manicured. He presented himself as a polite, well-educated, worldly gentleman.

Thomas studied Clarice carefully. He was a little riled that she wasn't showing any interest in him. She sat in the big leather chair, wishing her unwanted guest would disappear. Her dark, messy hair was twisted into an untidy knot that was about to come undone. Her saucer-like, soft brown eyes belied her intelligence and energy. Her dark complexion set her apart from the typical snow-white icy debutantes presented at court. Clarice was exotic, and every caramel curve of her body filled men with the desire to be her lover.

She'd not noticed that two buttons were missing from her magenta bodice. Thomas McGill couldn't move his eyes away from the small piece of flesh that was protruding. Her skirt was rich gold and reached her ankles which revealed boots that were made for walking. She was wrapped up in a bright shawl, a masterpiece of velvet and silk patches sewn together. The colours were rich shades of scarlet, magenta, emerald, sapphire, and turquoise. It was edged with a gold fringe that glittered in the firelight. Her mother had told her she looked hideous, and all the fair, English maidens pulled up their noses when they saw her.

Thomas didn't leave the library, preferring to have a stab at small talk, but Clarice wasn't in the mood to listen. She answered him only to be polite. But, as men often are, the more she tried to avoid him, the more he pursued her.

After some time, Thomas McGill chose to be candid.

"Miss Lawrence," he said boldly, "may I take you to tea next Saturday afternoon?"

"I have an appointment next Saturday afternoon," she answered truthfully. "I am sorry."

"Another time, perhaps?" came the crestfallen reply.

*

Thomas was smitten by Clarice. He'd never met anyone like her before. She'd not revealed much of her personal life except that she lived in her own lodgings and attended a London university. McGill had no qualms with women studying, as long as it was something 'useful.' For him, 'useful' meant subjects like music, art and literature—topics that were 'uplifting' and 'of great cultural benefit.'

*

Three weeks passed, yet Thomas, a cad who usually lost interest in women quickly, couldn't forget Clarice. While on his way to an afternoon card game, he stopped at the post office, wrote a quick note, and dropped it into the big red pillar box. It was a letter to Clarice inviting her to Claridge's for luncheon the following Saturday. Clarice didn't respond, not to him at least. However, she did throw the note into the fire with glee.

It took six weeks, and a lot of grovelling before Thomas McGill finally secured an appointment with Clarice Lawrence. She agreed to go for a stroll with him in Hyde Park and planned to be so actively disagreeable that he would never ask her out again.

3

THE SNUB

The following Saturday, the unlikely twosome met in Hyde Park as planned. He arrived at the West Gate in a small buggy. A carriage stopped behind him, and Clarice watched Lady Martha Lawrence and Lady McGill climb out. They would chaperone their adult children through the formal gardens. Clarice wondered if her mother was afraid that she would lose her virginity under a lavender bush.

Lady McGill had to concede that Clarice Lawrence was different to the other women whom Thomas had tried to court, and she was doubtful that she would make an acceptable partner for her son. Martha Lawrence, on the other hand, had no time to think of anything but herself and was far too busy ingratiating herself with Lady McGill.

"You have raised your daughter very well, Martha. She has grace and poise," Lady McGill lied while she studied Clarice's strange clothing and worn shoes.

"Oh, thank you, my dear."

Clarice's mother smiled from ear to ear.

"Such grace and poise," Lady McGill praised before secretly shaking her head and looking sour.

Martha wondered if the woman was blind. Clarice had arrived in one of her ridiculous outfits, looking like she'd stepped out of a cow shed in Romania.

"I believe that Clarice lives in the city, which is ideal for courting, is it not?"

Lady McGill was an expert at mining for information.

"I believe so," said Martha, who would not disagree with anything.

"It must be lovely having her so close to you. I am sure you get very lonely in that big house."

"She isn't living with me. She has lodgings of her own. She is most independent," Martha answered, hoping that it would impress the woman.

"I must invite her to bridge one afternoon. It is a wonderful way to introduce her to our circle. Does she play?"

"She would be delighted to play bridge with you. However, you may need to give her sufficient notice," Martha said without thinking.

"Why is that, my dear? Does she support a charity that keeps her busy?"

Martha hoped that the truth would impress Lady McGill.

"Clarice attends London University," Martha said with a big, false smile which quickly faded.

"What?" Lady McGill exclaimed. "How ridiculous. Education is wasted on a woman."

Martha quickly changed tack.

"Of course, I told her that. I would have never allowed it, you see. But my husband insisted she be educated."

"Your husband agreed to her preposterous plan?"

"I said the very same thing to Frank. I warned *'it gives her ideas above her station.'*"

"What is she doing there? Literature? Poetry? Art? Something useful, I hope."

Martha swallowed.

"Ancient History and Egyptology," she stammered.

"Oh, my dear Martha. I am so sorry for you. You must be at your wit's end. Please don't tell me that Clarice has been caught up in this common Bohemian lifestyle that everybody is so intrigued with. The Pre-Raphaelite brotherhood has a lot to answer for. They opened Pandora's box and filled people's heads with gibberish."

"Excuse me?" Martha was confused.

"Where is her apartment situated, my dear?" Lady McGill asked, a coldness creeping into her voice.

"Chelsea."

Lady McGill didn't say anything for some time. Her jaw visibly clenched.

"Just as I expected! Chelsea is a pit of inequity. There are clubs on almost every corner. Actually, it's not a pit—it's a 'cesspit'. Riddled with lazy, artistic, and liberal political types. You do know they believe in premarital relationships and living in sin? Who knows who she has been involved with?"

Lady McGill continued to divulge more details of this hedonistic lifestyle as if she'd personally experienced the hell and vice. Martha was troubled yet impressed with Lady McGill's detailed knowledge of this strange nonconformist culture.

"Chelsea is the equivalent of Paris's Montmartre. Goodness me—it only lacks the Moulin Rouge and that gaudy windmi—."

Lady McGill stopped mid-sentence and cleared her throat. Then, looking straight into Martha's eyes, she delivered the body blow.

> "Martha, you know you are a very dear friend, but I must be direct. We are not looking for our son to marry someone with Clarice's, err—let's say—*'qualities.'* We would prefer someone of the same social standing as Thomas. Old money, you might say. We would never accept a woman who runs around looking at pyramids and those dreadful mummies. And as for her attire, well, it is beyond bizarre."

> "Yes, I am sure we can do something about that," Martha muttered. "A trip to Harrod's, and she will soon scrub up, I'm sure."

Inside though, Martha was seething. Her stubborn daughter had chosen a deeply embarrassing lifestyle. She'd warned Frank that he would rue the day he allowed Clarice to attend university. How those words were coming home to roost.

Martha would never forgive Frank or Clarice for embarrassing her. Moreover, Lady McGill had made it clear that she didn't consider the Lawrences to be in the same class as her noble family. Defeated and furious, Dame Martha felt like all her years of brown-nosing social climbing had been for nothing. Her title was all for show and impressed no one of real substance.

It wasn't only Martha who was enraged. Thomas McGill was too. The spoilt young man wasn't used to hearing the word 'no'.

"I will see Clarice Lawrence whenever I wish," he yelled at his mother.

"She is not a free spirit. She is a foolish girl who delights in bringing disgrace to her family—and she will certainly disgrace ours—"

"Mother!"

"No, Thomas. I don't want to hear another word. You will not meet with Clarice again."

In the corner of the drawing-room was Lord McGill reading The Times.

"Oh, do stop the shouting," said Lord McGill, collapsing the newspaper onto his lap. "You are both being ridiculous."

"He has to obey us. We will not have some common trollop wreck our family name," the lady of the house protested.

"Wife," he barked back, "leave the boy alone. Allow him to have some fun and sow his wild oats. He will lose interest as soon as he has bedded her."

Lady McGill gasped at his crude and offensive remarks.

> "For heaven's sake, woman," shouted Lord
> McGill, "stop being such a prude. No wonder
> we only have one child."

This time, Thomas's jaw dropped. Such matters were never even hinted at in company and never in front of one's children. Lady McGill blushed scarlet.

> "Damn it," Lord McGill cursed, "her father is as
> wealthy as a Rothchild. She will arrive with
> money. God knows we could do with a lot
> more of that—new or old! Your antics are
> costing me a fortune!"

Lord McGill strode across to her, holding his reddening face inches from hers, arms flailing ever more wildly with every syllable.

> "Can you not see how much you overindulge
> our son? Sponsoring his every whim and
> fancy in a desperate attempt to get him
> married. I am sure we've spent more than
> sending the most self-absorbed of Macaronis
> on a six-month grand tour of Europe!"

Lord McGill collapsed back in his chair, exhausted. Perspiration dripped off his bright pink face. His wife looked at him with utter disdain. How deeply unattractive he was. After giving him a son, Lady McGill had deliberately frozen him out of her bed. She deplored him.

4

MAKING ENDS MEET

Darlene Cornish was a much sought after 'tart', and she earned an honest living in the old and established profession of prostitution. Her sensational assets could have gained her a position in the finest brothels of the city, but she'd no ambition. Instead, she preferred to tell people that she had a job at the Prince Edward Hotel, working as a barmaid.

The Prince Edward Hotel consisted of a busy pub downstairs with lodgings upstairs. It had once been a quaint sweet shop, and its cheerful owners had lived in the rooms above. The building was sold and transformed into the Prince Edward Tavern, then the hotel. It soon became the home of vagabonds and wealthy men. Both types of men liked Darlene to fulfil their darkest desires.

Over time, she'd told so many people that she was a barmaid that she actually began to believe the lie herself. Unfortunately for her, many witnesses could attest to her generosity with her body. So, the only person Darlene managed to fool was herself.

She fell pregnant young, at the tender age of fifteen. Nine months later, she gave birth to a baby boy. Darlene had no interest in the child other than occasionally feeding him if no one else would.

Darlene lived in a dream world. Her surname wasn't Cornish but Lawrence. She was the daughter of a farmer up north. She'd decided she couldn't bear the idea of milking cows and churning butter for the rest of her life. So, she packed her bags, took her savings, and caught the train to London. She was of the naïve opinion that if she deployed her powers correctly, she could meet someone from the middle class, make him fall in love with her and live happily ever after.

Arriving in London with very little money, within a week, she was broke. It took her ten days without shelter and four days without food to prostitute herself to the first chap who approached her. The experience was vile, and so was the man she slept with. That said, Darlene could justify her behaviour. It was a temporary solution to secure her big step up in life. Each time, she reminded herself that she'd earned enough for a bed to sleep in and a plate of food. But, alas, Darlene's meagre earnings were only enough to sustain her for one night. The following evening, she was forced to sell herself to another man.

Darlene promised herself that she would only do it until she got a real job. She was as good as her word and soon found a position washing floors at a warehouse in

Wapping. Unfortunately, her first wage packet was a great disappointment. She'd earned more money as a prostitute than she did in a legitimate job. She stared at the single coin in her palm. Then, she threw down her mop in an almighty rage and quit on the spot.

Darlene went back to the streets and her old job. As time went on, she became savvier and soon made a lot more money, but that didn't change the most important thing. Her working conditions were still appalling—not just the job, but the workplace itself. She walked the streets and had to be content with performing her services in dark alleyways and seedy rooms. However, she did still have one asset at her disposal. She was still young and pretty, which was how she got Benny Hobson's attention.

> "Come and work with me, lass," he told her
> kindly, "I will give you a bit of a job as a
> barmaid. There are rooms where you can do
> your business. We are one big happy family
> down there. You will be alright."

Benny was a good sort. He was kind, generous and protective. Benny never took advantage of the ladies who lived, lurked and worked in the rooms above the pub. It was simple economics. The busier the women were, the busier the pub was.

Darlene reinvented herself. She changed her name from Lawrence to Cornish. It was the name of a client who had once been very gentle and kind to her. He only acquired her services twice, and she'd fallen in love with him. Changing her name to Cornish gave birth to the fantasy that he'd married her and had departed on a long journey. Patrons never gave their real names to prostitutes, but Darlene refused to believe that the man had lied to her.

Darlene chose to include the child in her fantasy. She believed that she'd conceived Joey on Mr Cornish's last visit with her. She would never forget that day. It had been a beautiful afternoon and the first and only time a man had ever made love to her.

In the summer of 1889, Darlene carried the child from Whitechapel to Spitalfields to register his birth. She would call him Joseph Charles Cornish and named his father Charles David Cornish.

The registry office stood in a narrow street littered with rough types who had fallen short of the law. She stood in a long row of people who had come to document the birth of their children. They all looked haggard and desperate.

Darlene was the youngest mother in the queue, so some men poked fun at her, while others recognised her from The Prince Edward. Her humiliation grew when she heard women gossiping about her and her line of work.

"Do you know the father then, lass?" asked a man who frequented the tavern. "Does he

look like his father? That might give you a
clue, eh?"

The men around her guffawed.

No sooner did the men stop than the women began. A
drawn woman in her early twenties had a go next. She
had four children hanging on her skirts and a baby in
her arms. All her teeth were gone.

"You will be like me soon," she cackled.

The other women began cackling, too, delighted that
another woman had been baptised into their club of
despair.

*

"Joseph Charles Cornish," said Darlene.

"Are you sure?" asked the clerk. "Where is the
father? Are you married? Where is your
marriage certificate?"

The grilling continued.

"Look, Miss," said the clerk.

"Mrs Cornish," Darlene corrected him.

"Where is his father?"

"He is at sea."

"A lot of fathers are at sea."

"Don't you get clever with me," Darlene spat across the counter. "My husband isn't any old sailor. He is an officer. He is the captain of a mail ship."

The clerk sighed. He looked over Darlene's head and saw a queue of approximately fifty people behind her.

"Very well then—Mrs—Cornish. Make up a date so we can get on with this."

He completed the task and handed Darlene the birth certificate. If he had one case like Darlene a day, he had a hundred.

5

JOEY'S EDUCATION

Every Sunday morning, Joey would visit Eliza O'Shea. They had been meeting since the lad was six years old. Eliza lived above the *Keg and Crown* in Spitalfields. Joey didn't know where Eliza came from. All he knew was that she was the kindest person in the world.

Eliza had developed a soft spot for Joey when she'd worked as a barmaid with his mother. There was something about the boy that filled her with hope. He had a twinkle in his eye, quick wit and good humour, which would be his saving grace. He was a little cheeky, somewhat shrewd, and highly creative. Eliza studied his broad smile, bright eyes and the shock of fair hair that hung over them.

While Darlene was entertaining a client, Eliza kept the boy occupied. She soon realised that the little boy had a keen mind. Every time that Joey was with her, she would teach him something. One day she called him aside and instructed him to be at her room by nine o'clock every Sunday morning. But on the first Sunday after their conversation, he stayed as far away from Eliza as possible. He'd no intention of going to church with her.

"Where were you, young man?" Eliza demanded.

"I was very busy," said Joey.

"Busy with shenanigans," Eliza accused him.

Joey eventually brushed up the courage to voice his concern.

"Eliza, are you going to take me to church?"

"What?" Eliza shrieked with delight. "I don't think that there is a church who wants the likes of me."

"If it isn't that, then what?" he demanded stubbornly.

"You should be in the Ragged School, my boy."

"I am not going there. I am not a little kid anymore, and they laugh at me. I can't read and write, and those wee blokes can."

"Do you want them to laugh at you forever? If you can count money, you can do numbers. Reading is easy. Letters are just squiggles that make up words. When you understand how the squiggle sounds, it all makes sense."

"You promise you won't take me to Sunday School?"

"I promise, but you have to learn, and I will teach you."

Early the following Sunday, Eliza heard a knock at her door. She was delighted to find Joey on her doorstep, and they had never missed a Sunday meeting since then. Eliza was the closest friend that Joey would ever have, and she was more important to him than his mother ever could be.

It was on one of these Sundays' that Eliza surprised him. She'd been to the market and bought him new clothes.

"These are for going out in, Joey."

Joey cocked his head to one side and frowned.

"Is that for school?" he asked.

Eliza said nothing. Joey folded his arms and sat on the side of her bed. He looked at his worn shoes and felt glum. He knew that sooner or later, Eliza would insist that he go to school.

"Eliza, I told you I am never going to that horrid school."

"Get washed up and put on them new rags. We are going to town."

"To the city? On a Sunday?"

"Yes, lad. Get on with it."

Joey put on his new outfit. The trousers fit perfectly, and the coat was warm. He wiggled his toes inside his new shoes, so much roomier than his old hand-me-downs.

She smoothed down his wayward hair, plonked a flat cap on his head, and straightened his collar.

"Now, you look like a gentleman. A real bobby dazzler."

Eliza didn't look too bad herself. Exchanging her shiny red crinoline dress for a simple cotton frock with pink flowers, she seemed almost normal.

"There is only one rule, Joey," Eliza told him firmly. "Don't speak loudly. The posh folks don't care for the likes of us, so we must mind our P's and Q's. Today we will walk through London, and I will show you everything I can remember."

"You are posh, Eliza. You always sound posh."

"Thank you, Joey. I will accept that as a compliment," Eliza answered with a twinkle in her eye.

Eliza showed Joey as much of London as she could manage in one Sunday afternoon. His new (to him) shoes rubbed his feet almost raw, but he didn't care.

"Did you enjoy yourself today?" Eliza asked when they got back to her room.

"Oh, Eliza!" Joey exclaimed. "It was magnificent!"

Eliza looked down and smiled. She'd made the boy happy. After all the years of living in the dark confines of the Keg and Crown, Eliza had found joy and purpose in helping the lad, and it gave her a joyous feeling to see him so excited.

A month later, Eliza took a day off from work under the auspices of visiting the doctor. She and Joey put on their good clothes and headed to the city once more.

> "You need to be a gentleman, Joey. We are going to a fascinating place today, and they will toss us on the street if we act common."

Joey giggled. He imagined the two of them on the pavement licking their wounds after a good walloping.

> "I will be a gentleman, I promise."

Eliza took him to Great Russell Street in London. As the saying goes, it was the first day of the rest of Joey's life. From the moment he stepped into the British Museum, he knew that this was where he wanted to work forever, and he told Eliza just that.

Instead of telling him that there was no hope for a boy from Whitechapel to work in such a great museum, Eliza told him that he could achieve anything if he worked hard enough.

Eliza didn't realise how powerful her words were. She'd given Joey a dream that he could work toward. It was also a dream that would comfort him when he felt despair.

"Eliza," said Joey while they walked home,
"how do you know so much about London and
the museum?"

Eliza didn't answer immediately. Instead, she looked straight ahead. Then she realised where she was and that Joey was still there.

"I was once married to a very important man.
When he decided that he didn't want me
anymore, I had no money, and I came to live
here."

*

Joey made his way back to the room that he and his mother shared in Dorset Street. He could see the window from where he stood. His mother had pasted old newspapers against the window panes for privacy. Unfortunately, it served little purpose as Joey could still see the silhouettes of his mother and Hector when the lamp was lit. He dared not nor desired to go back until he saw Hector leave.

Joey was under strict instructions not to bother his mother while she was entertaining. She told him that Hector gave her money and didn't want to jeopardise her income with Joey hanging around her. Hector had no time for Joey. The boy was too bright and independent for his years, and he made Hector feel like an idiot.

Joey despised Hector, and it was the only time that his humour failed him. His mother was no better. No sooner had thoughts of his mother entered his mind than he suppressed them. His mind skipped back to Eliza. He would work towards his dream. He wouldn't live in Whitechapel forever.

*

One night Darlene and Hector were talking, and Joey overheard the conversation.

"We need to leave here, Darlene," said Hector.

"Why are you saying all that now, Heck?"

"Things are upside down in the business, love. If we don't get out of London, the coppers are going to find me. If anybody speaks out about the death of Richie Roberts, I'm going to find myself at the end of a rope," Hector told her.

"Where would we go? Asked Darlene.

"We can go anywhere, my love. We just need to get away from England. Ships are leaving Southampton all the time. I have enough money to take us to America or South Africa. We can go to Singapore. Wherever you want to live, we can get there."

Darlene smiled from ear to ear. The idea of living in America appealed to her greatly. People got rich in America.

"Oh, my Angel," cried Darlene. "What I would give to go and live in America!"

Her eyes moved towards Joey, sitting quietly in the corner.

"What about him then?"

"I'm not bloody dragging him with us," Hector swore. "He knows how to look after himself. Too bloody clever for his own good sometimes. He doesn't need you anymore, darling. He'll get by. You don't have to worry about anything."

So, Darlene listened to Hector, and he booked a passage on a ship which would sail from Southampton to Sydney. Darlene and Hector left on a bright Tuesday morning. They were full of enthusiasm for the new life that lay ahead.

6

THE DEPARTURE

Joey was too busy running numbers for Mr Chang, the Chinese bookmaker, to realise that his mother had taken a train to Southampton with Hector, and from there, would go on to Sydney.

By now, Joey had an illustrious career as a runner for Mr Chang, who ran a Fafi game from his kitchen door. Although Joey had purchased himself an old top hat at the marketplace, he'd decided that he needed to look more sophisticated when he did his job. As he chased up and down the dirty streets, he soon earned the nickname 'Joey Top Hat.' Joey's job entailed collecting bets, giving the odds, and avoiding the police. By 1900 gambling was legal as long as bookies paid tax. However, Mr Chang refused to pay tax and ran his illegal betting business out of his kitchen.

Mr Chang had been in desperate need of a runner. The lad he employed had to be quick enough to outrun the police because Mr Chang didn't need the coppers at his door confiscating his hard-earned money. Also, the lad would have to be good at numbers, have a good memory and be honest. Beyond that, Mr Chang needed somebody who wouldn't blabber his business all over

London. It was difficult to find anyone who had all five qualities.

Mr and Mrs Chang were warm, charming people, and the atmosphere in their home was peaceful. However, they were appalled to hear that Darlene had left her son to survive by himself in Whitechapel. The area was fraught with criminal sorts, filthy, and rife with disease.

Mr Chang didn't consider gambling immoral. On the contrary, he thought he was giving local punters the opportunity to invest and grow their wealth.

In his broken English, he explained that gambling was the same as trading on the London Stock Market.

"Economics, Joey. Chinese good at numbers."

The great difference was that Mr Chang's investors could gamble with less money, and the earnings could be way more profitable than a bank would guarantee. The winnings didn't hinge on the price of gold and the erratic global markets. Both banking and gambling were a risk.

"Me velly, velly, sorry for Joey," Mr Chang told him.

"Your mudda done bad thing leaving you. I pay you good. I feed you good. Joey sleep in Mr Chang's house. Joey sleep in store, and you pay Mrs Chang."

Joey was ahead of the game. He suggested to Mr Chang that he preferred to be paid a percentage of the business he brought in.

Mr Chang was caught off guard. The boy had a quick mind. Mr Chang knew it was precisely what he would have chosen to do if he was Joey. It would be more viable than getting a weekly wage. Soon Joey became a well-known figure in Whitechapel, and his clientele trusted him more than they did Mr Chang.

After a few days, Mr Chang had to sit down with Joey. He explained how the game worked.

"Joey, I velly concern," said Mr Chang. "You are no good for business."

"I pay you too good, Joey, you know, good for business. You tell tluth too much. If you no listen, you go out of Mr Chang's house."

Joey frowned. He was in no mind to ruin his hard-earned reputation because Mr Chang wanted him to cheat.

"I won't be a crook, Mr Chang," said Joey.

He knew Mr Chang would be very angry with him, so he tried to reason with the man.

"Nobody trusts you, Mr Chang. If I cheat, they will never place a bet with me again," Joey told him firmly.

Mr Chang was surprised by Joey's cheek. He muttered under his breath in Mandarin, wishing that he could strangle the little swine. But reality soon replaced the red mist. He knew that if he murdered Joey, he would hang for the crime. Finally, he came to his senses and told himself that Joey wasn't worth it.

Eventually, Mr Chang's greed got the better of him, and he began to yell at the top of his lungs.

"Joey, you go now! No more food! No more bed! Mr Chang velly lich. Joey is velly poor. Joey go now!"

Mrs Chang was a different kettle of fish. She stared at the ragged little boy, her face like thunder, the blood visibly pulsing in her neck. She pulled her finger across her throat.

"Mrs Chang no want Joey. Mrs Chang slit Joey thloat like a dog. I cook you like a cat. Mrs Chang eat you like pig."

Joey's eyes stretched to the size of saucers. The little woman was vicious. He knew he would be done for if he didn't get away quickly. Joey turned and ran. He dodged chimes and red lanterns until he found the front door. Joey ran without ceasing until he was far beyond the Chinese section of Whitechapel. Eventually, he collapsed in a heap on the steps of a doorway, unable to run anymore.

Suddenly the fear became relief, then euphoria. Joey exploded into gales of laughter. He recalled Mrs Chang's face as she threatened to cook him. He'd never heard that sort of menace before.

His breath began to return to its normal rhythm. He stared into thin air, lost in his own thoughts. Little did anyone know that the boy was formulating his next business plan. He stood up and tried to make himself look decent by putting on his top hat.

*

Joey jauntily changed direction and began walking towards Spitalfields. It was time to speak to Eliza.

"I don't know, Joey. What do I know about betting?"

"Eliza, think about it, please. I know you hate working at the Keg. Perhaps we can change all that."

Eliza knew that Joey was right, but she wasn't prone to having young boys dictating her future. It jangled her nerves, but she gave the suggestion a lot of thought.

"You need a place to live, I expect, Joe?"

"Fear not, I have a place. I have places all over here, in fact."

He made a wide arc with his hand.

"I don't just mean a roof over your head. I mean with someone to care for you."

"I can care for myself," Joey said with a pout.

There was a long pause whilst each one ruminated on their situation. Eliza spoke first.

"Alright, Joey. I will agree to your plan on one condition."

Joey raised an eyebrow questioningly.

"We must share a room."

What? He'd not expected that. The news made his heart leap, and his smile stretched from ear to ear.

"Yes, Eliza, that is what I thought as well."

"Don't lie, yer little sod."

Joey began to tell Eliza how it would all work. By the end of the evening, all the details had been thrashed out. They decided that Eliza would start selling old clothing at the market, and Joey would run the bets. The pair were the most unlikely bookmakers in the East End.

Joey and Eliza excelled. They could afford a two-roomed place. Joey was overwhelmed when he climbed onto an old beat-up cot bed in the warm shelter of their tiny home. It was the first time in his life that he felt he'd had a real home. A warm, safe haven where he could eat and sleep in a modicum of comfort. Their (albeit unorthodox) partnership thrived. Eliza ran the household, and Joey brought in the business.

There was only one problem—they were doing too well.

"We are going to be robbed, Joey. The louts know that I have a lot of money at the stall. I am scared they will put a knife to my throat one evening."

Joey was deeply distressed. It was only money, and he would rather give away everything they owned than have something terrible happen to Eliza.

"I'll make a plan for us, Eliza," Joey told her with dotormination.

"We need to put this money in a bank."

"Then let's do that then."

"You don't understand. Women cannot open an account by themselves. They need their husband's permission."

"Then we must find you a husband, lovely lady!" laughed Joey.

Eliza pulled a horrid face to make herself as unattractive as possible.

"Who would want this?" she rasped.

By now, Joey was gasping for breath between the chuckles.

"Then I shall open the account."

"You can't, you daft thing. The clerk will see you're too young a mile off."

"That is thoroughly unacceptable," protested Joey, keen to show off his command of bigger words.

"Yes, it's a bloody disgrace if you ask me."

The laughter subsided, and silence reigned again.

"Listen, Eliza, I have an idea."

"What is it?"

Joey didn't reply, too busy putting on his top hat and heading for the door.

"Where you off to, now?"

"I think I know someone who can help us."

"Is he trustworthy?"

"I hope so," the boy answered.

With that, he dashed out of the front door, leaving a bewildered Eliza watching him go.

*

Joey went straight to Raffi Fischer's office. Everybody knew the moneylender, one of the most notorious figures in Spitalfields. The wheeler-dealer was badly received in his own community, and Rabbi Solavitch was at the end of his tether.

"There are better ways to make a living, Raffi," said the old, bearded man.

"Don't be troubled, rabbi. I am helping the community. I perform mitzvah every day. Who will lend out money to these poor souls if I do not?"

Raffi gave his best smile in an attempt to placate the rabbi.

"No, Raffi," he sighed, his frustration growing. "It isn't a mitzvah if you make them pay interest. You have to give it to them—unconditionally."

Raffi took out his fob watch and studied the time, hoping the rabbi would take it as a cue to leave. However, Rabbi Solavitch had no intention of going anywhere. He'd known Raffi since he was born.

"Stop charging these poor people interest, Raffi. Stop harassing them till they pay you. You are not allowed to demand the money back. You have patience for seven years, and if they don't pay, you write off their debt. It is a mitzvah. These people struggle, Raffi. You have more than they do."

Raffi wanted to leave but dared not turn his back on the rabbi.

"I am going now," said Rabbi Solavitch,
putting on his hat. "Get an honest job, Raffi.
You make the whole community look like
greedy sharks."

Raffi looked at the floor, feeling ashamed and annoyed at the same time.

"You need to think about Rebecca and your
sons. Their souls rest in your hands."

Raffi thanked the rabbi for a visit but was relieved to see him go. He made a lot of money and would not sacrifice his lucrative business because of a simple visit. As far as he was concerned, times had changed. He'd been ostracised by his orthodox community. Eventually, he gave up living in the Jewish Quarter of Whitechapel, which made his father-in-law furious. He found a comfortable apartment on the peripheries of the East End and tried to ignore his faith.

*

There was a loud, determined knock on the office door. Rebecca Fischer opened the door and looked at the urchin in front of her.

"Yes?" she said, frowning down at the boy.

"I want to see Mr Fischer, please?"

"Why?"

"It's business."

Rebecca was very busy. Raffi had been in a foul mood since Rabbi Solavitch left, and he'd ordered her around all morning. Raffi's grizzling was contagious, and she was fed up. If Rebecca had felt better, she would have interrogated Joey for all his details and been a better 'gatekeeper.' Instead, she invited the lad inside and showed him into Raffi's office.

"You have a client," said Rebecca, in a matter-of-fact tone.

She pushed Joey towards a chair, and he sat down

Raffi looked the boy up and down, and his gaze was naturally drawn to the hat.

"You must be Joey Tophat, then," said Raffi. "I have been waiting to meet you. I believe that you are a runner for Mr Chang's Fafi game."

Joey gave him a wide grin.

"I don't work for Mr Chang no more. He sacked me."

"I don't do business with children," said Mr Fischer, in a robust Yiddish accent.

"I know, but I am different. All I ask is a moment of your time," Joey answered politely.

Eliza had taught him to behave like a gentleman, and now that training was paying off. The old moneylender was trying to pick up on the real reason for Joey's visit and calculating the risk of loaning Joey money. Joey had made quite a name for himself in the East End. The only way he would work out what the boy really wanted was to carry on the conversation.

"Shall we start again? How can I help you?" Raffi asked, stony-faced.

Joey wasn't intimidated. On the contrary, he was calm, confident, and above all, remembering to be polite.

"I have a proposition for you."

"I said, I don't lend money to children," Raffi said gruffly.

"Mr Fischer," said Joey confidently, "hear me out. And before you tell me a third time, I promise you—I have no need of a loan."

Mr Fischer almost fell off his chair. He looked at Joey and frowned.

Raffi Fischer wondered how a street urchin could have an offer for him. He'd been so confident that Joey was approaching him for a loan, and now he was confused.

"Shall we get down to business? What is it that you want from me, Mr Tophat?"

Raffi decided it would be best to speak to the lad like he would to any adult standing before him.

"I need to open an account with you, sir."

"A bank account?" said Mr Fischer, perplexed. "But, I am a lender, not a bank."

Mr Fischer had never encountered a child like this before and remained cautious. You never knew when someone was spying on your business in the semi-lawless East End. Surely, nobody would send a child to spy on him? Would they?

"Go ahead, Mr Tophat. Tell me what you have in mind."

"Sir, I am just a young boy. No bank in this city will allow me to deposit my money with them."

"Well, why do you need an account?" Mr Fischer blurted out. "Can't you just put it under your mattress like a normal lad? A piggy bank?"

"You don't understand, Mr Fischer. I have a lot of money, and I need to put it somewhere safe."

"What makes you think I can help you?" Mr Fischer barked.

"It's very straightforward. I know you have a lot of money in the bank—and I need you to keep mine with yours."

"Well, you'd better tell me more about how you amassed this money of yours."

The lad filled in the gaps between the hearsay and myths Raffi had heard about 'Joey Tophat' and the truth. He described his partnership with Eliza O'Shea, how she'd been helping him with his education, and how her help had turned him into the canny lad he'd become. Fischer couldn't believe his ears. He didn't even have grown men who would dare to approach him as blatantly as this boy.

Mr Fischer nodded slowly, uncertain where the conversation was leading, mainly because the name O'Shea sounded familiar, and so it should. Dennis O'Shea was Minister for Economics, a prominent politician who had recently divorced his wife, Lizelle, for her supposed adultery. The scandal had rocked the upper classes, more so when it became clear Dennis O'Shea's lover was waiting in the wings. He remarried within weeks of his divorce being approved in parliament. People began to wonder who was at fault in the breakdown of their marriage—and it probably wasn't Lizelle.

Nobody knew where the former Mrs O'Shea had disappeared to. There was a rumour that she'd gone overseas. But, all that time, Eliza was in Spitalfields.

It was dawning on Raffi that Joey's Eliza was also a well-educated woman with a good head on her shoulders who had 'learned a lot from her husband.' Raffi was impressed. If Eliza was Lizelle as he suspected, Joey Tophat was in good hands indeed.

*

"I don't work with a tenner here and tenner there, young man. I will only be interested if you have a considerable amount of cash."

Joey smiled. He had anticipated the question. He had an answer that would shock Mr Fischer to the core.

"Sir, I saved a couple of grand when I worked for Mr Chang. Eliza has about one hundred punters who bet against us every day."

"Every day?"

"Yes, sir."

Joey might have thought two thousand pounds was a considerable sum, but the wily moneylender wasn't impressed. He dealt in hundreds of thousands of pounds.

The only reason Fischer tolerated such a small fry suggestion was that he admired Joey's intelligence and tenacity. He wondered what had happened for the lad to be in this position. What impressed him was that an eight-year-old boy could make that amount of money all by himself. He wondered what else Joey and Eliza could achieve together.

"How will you pay your punters?" asked Mr Fischer.

"We'll manage the bets at the stall. Anyone with a big win comes here to collect their winnings, minus your cut for your trouble. If anything happens to me, I want Eliza to be alright."

Mr Fischer didn't want to make any quick decisions. The story was remarkable. In truth, the story was unbelievable. Yet, here was proof, in flesh and blood, that the tale was accurate. The figures stacked up.

Joey was expecting to shake hands on the deal when Raffi stood up, but he was wrong. Fischer put on a show of being gruff. He yelled for his wife to come into the room.

"Get him out of here. Now!"

Raffi Fischer turned to Joey as Rebecca grabbed him roughly by his skinny elbow.

"Get out of here and don't come back."

As the lad was yanked to his feet, he steadied his top hat with his free hand and glared at Fischer, now leaning back in his chair, ignoring him. Then, Joey was shoved onto the street, and the door slammed in his face shortly after.

Raffi was deep in thought and didn't stir for fifteen minutes. He'd never been put in such a situation before. He had no doubt that the youngster had something special about him. He was far more intelligent than his highly-educated sons. If he had to choose who to do business with, he would rather choose Joey over any family member. The thought was quite a revelation.

"Who was that little urchin?" Rebecca Fischer asked when she returned to his office.

"My dear, that is one of the most remarkable people I have ever met. His name is Joey Tophat, and he is going to be famous. I'm toying with him. He'll be back—and I'll be waiting."

He was right. Joey Tophat never accepted defeat. Five minutes later, Rebecca found herself letting the boy back in.

7

THE DAY EVERYTHING
CHANGED

The Daily Mirror had printed the headline in thick, sombre, black capitals.

'CASTLE LINER SINKS IN AUSTRALIAN WATERS'

The event was tragic enough, but the editor of the Mirror underlined the headline to reinforce the scale of the calamity.

Joey Tophat walked right past the news vendor with no interest in those headlines that morning. Some other headlines were of interest, though. He recently started to study horse racing and was on the hunt for the latest edition of Sportsman's magazine. It was Wednesday, and he was preparing for the midweek races at Aintree. A small group of bookies were friends, and every day they would meet to discuss the day's key races: the turf, the jockeys, the going, the trainers, and the stables. Most people couldn't afford to attend the race meetings, only to follow them, but Joey always went to the racecourse if there was a meeting close by. The bookies liked the lad's demeanour, so they went as far as meeting in a tearoom instead of the local pub to include him in the discussions.

After the meeting, Joey caught a second glimpse of the headlines. It was as if the huge letters were pursuing him wherever he went. Eventually, he stopped, bought a newspaper, and began reading about the sinking.

The mail ship had departed from Southampton and made for the Pacific. Two days from Sydney, the captain realised that the vessel was taking on water. The captain performed all the necessary safety procedures. He sealed off the bulkheads and was confident he would save the ship. The officers sent a message asking for assistance, and there should have been no fatalities. However, without any warning, the mild summer weather suddenly turned wild. Icy winds from the south rolled in. The cold front sank, displacing the warm air beneath it, and within no time, the ocean was whipped into a frenzy of salt and foam. There was no visibility. The fog lights on the bow and mast were defeated by the white cloud that enveloped them. The deep sound of the foghorn was lost to the raging wind. In the chaos of the elements, the ship collided with a fishing boat. Already at a disadvantage, the great vessel became unstable. The ballasts failed as the ship took on water. The great waves rolled it over, and within minutes it sank.

There were no survivors. Nobody had even had time to reach a lifeboat. Those who had jumped overboard had drowned. At the end of the article, it referred the reader to the list of souls who had perished. Joey turned to page two. The surnames were listed in alphabetical order. He didn't have to read far to see *'Cornish, Darlene'*.

Joey didn't know what to do, think or feel. He supposed he should feel crippling grief. But he wasn't. He'd not known his mother very well, and she'd never shown him kindness or been gentle towards him. One thing he did know was that he wouldn't miss her. She was a stranger to him.

*

Unfortunately, the Metropolitan Board also had a list of the dead and was legally obliged to contact all the next of kin in search of minors orphaned by the event. One week later, they found Darlene Cornish's information. Their preliminary research noted that she had a son, Joseph Charles. Darlene's card was filed with the other Ds in a varnished wooden drawer with a tiny dull brass handle on the front. Soon, Joey's information was sent to the correct department and then passed along to the men on the ground tasked with finding the bereaved.

If Joey had been aware that the state intended to put him in an orphanage, he would have been careful to avoid any strangers. He would have moved to a new location or changed his name. Joey prided himself in his independence, but that was useless if his dead mother had registered him as her child.

*

Joey and Eliza were still living cheek-by-jowl, close to the market where Eliza had the stall. It was early morning and still dark outside when they were startled by a loud banging on the door. Joey hopped off his bed, thinking it was likely a punter coming to place a bet before going off to work.

"Bloody hell, Joey. These blokes need to learn some manners. This is an ungodly hour."

Joey laughed loudly. He opened the door, smiling at Eliza's griping. But, instead of one of his regular punters, he faced two official-looking gentlemen.

"Joseph Cornish?" one of the men demanded.

On hearing the question, Eliza dashed to the door.

"Why are you looking for Mr Cornish?" Eliza demanded.

"We're not. We're looking for Master Cornish."

The other man then spoke up equally gruffly.

"It's quite simple. This lad here, was his mother's name Darlene Cornish?"

Joey's savviness evaporated. He answered without thinking.

"Yes," he confirmed.

"Come with us, please," the man ordered him without any explanation.

"You leave him alone," said Eliza. "He isn't going off with people I don't know!"

"We are from the parish workhouse. I'm Mr King, and this is Mr Rich," he pointed at his friend.

"Why must I go to a workhouse?" Joey pleaded, confused.

"Your mother is dead, and you cannot look after yourself. The orphanages are full, and the older children will be housed at the Workhouse."

"I have looked after myself since I was knee-high to you," declared Joey.

"He is under my guardianship. You can see the boy is well cared for," Eliza said. "Surely, that counts for something."

"It doesn't, Ma'am. You may contact the authorities and speak to them if you wish to pursue formal guardianship."

Eliza shook her head disbelievingly.

*

Joey watched the two men. He knew he would have to escape somehow, but they were much bigger than him and rather official, faceless and frightening. His mind was a mess with thoughts. He had to get away or be locked up in a dreaded workhouse for what felt like forever to someone so young. What were his options? He could run to a friend's dingy lodgings in another sprawling rookery and hide away. It would take them months to find him in the maze of Whitechapel tenements, and he knew some places were so rough the average bobby was too scared to enter. On the other hand, he and Eliza could go and live somewhere far away. Australia? South Africa? Eliza could adopt him. But that would take months, and until then, he would be trapped.

Mr King had a stiff, aggressive posture and stood with his arms folded and his feet shoulder-width apart. He was too busy arguing with Eliza to pay attention to the lad.

It was a split-second decision. Joey shot forward like a bullet, dived onto his stomach and slid through Mr King's legs. Mr Rich spun around, utterly confused by what had just happened. Joey tore down the path and escaped into the street. The two officials chased after him. They were used to children trying to escape the system, and Joey wasn't the first brat they would have to catch. Behind them came Eliza, terrified of what they would do to Joey when they caught him.

Without thinking, Joey turned into a street that had a dead end. His little legs were tiring as he heard two grown men's footsteps catching up with him. He looked over his shoulder to see just where they were, and with that, he ran slap bang into a mountain of a man, Constable Milner.

"Why Joey, what's the hurry, son?" the policeman asked in a friendly manner.

"Constable," panted Joey, "those blokes want to cart me off to the workhouse! Cos my ma's—"

"I am sorry, lad. I know your mum died. It's a terrible blow for you, I'm sure."

"They are going to take me away, sir. Some pen pushers."

"I can't help you, Joey. You know the law. I can lose my job if I hide you. I would like to, but I can't risk it."

Constable Milner felt terrible saying the words.

"Don't worry about that, sir," said Joey. "I need you to do something for me, please? Please!"

"What is that?"

Constable Milner studied Joey's face.

"Sir, please go to Raffi Fischer over in Spitalfields."

"Why, lad? Do you owe him money?"

"No. Please, just ask Mr Fischer to look after Eliza. He will know what to do."

"But," stammered Constable Milner.

> "He will know what to do, sir. Eliza will need help, and Mr Fischer knows that he can trust me to repay him for his efforts."

Constable Milner was surprised. He knew that Joey Tophat took bets on the gee-gees but was unaware of the extent.

> "Promise me!" the boy insisted.

> "I promise. I will go straight there after my shift."

> "Thank you! Thank you, sir," Joey sighed with relief.

By now, the men had caught up with Joey. He suspected these two thugs might have given him a good beating if he'd not been with Constable Milner.

> "Do you know this boy?" Mr King barked at the officer.

> "Mind your manners, young man," Constable Milner said firmly. "May I remind you, you are talking to a policeman."

> "Who is this child?" asked Mr Rich.

"People call him Joey Tophat, and he is an upstanding member of the community," replied the constable.

"Tophat is an odd name," muttered Mr King. "Can you confirm his mother is Darlene Cornish?"

Milner nodded.

Mr Rich clamped a hand on the boy's shoulder and squeezed it until Joey crumpled in agony.

"The fact is your mother is dead, lad. We have been instructed by the government to get you off the streets and into the workhouse. You look like a ragamuffin. You are lucky that her majesty is prepared to accommodate you. A boy like you would starve to death on the street in a week. You should be grateful—"

"—grateful!" Joey whimpered in protest as he was frogmarched off.

"Yes. And don't try and escape," added Mr King, "or we'll wallop you. Your copper friend isn't with you now."

*

Raffi Fischer never enjoyed the police visiting him. Rebecca opened his office door and ushered Milner in. Raffi wondered what he'd done.

Raffi looked at his wife and his forehead creased. She looked at him and shrugged her shoulders.

"You can relax, Mr Fischer," said Constable Milner, "I am not here on official business."

Raffi smiled and shook the policeman's hand.

"What is your business, sir," asked Raffi in his deep, barely understandable Yiddish accent.

"Joey Tophat has asked me to give you a message. He is worried about Eliza O'Shea and asks if you would keep an eye on her. His punters need to collect their winnings, I suspect, and he needs your help."

Raffi listened to the constable, all the while shaking his head and smiling. One thing was certain—Joey Tophat was loyal.

"Thank you for delivering the message, Constable Milner. Please don't worry about anything. Joey Tophat is young, but he is honourable. I shall attend to Mrs O'Shea on Mr Tophat's behalf."

Sat alone in his office, Fischer smiled again. The walking cash-generating machine that was Joey Tophat now owed him a favour.

8

THE WORKHOUSE

Joey stood in the massive entrance of the workhouse orphanage wing and looked around him. There was absolutely nothing of colour in the large portal, only different shades of grey. The paint on the walls and floors was old and chipping. The furniture was threadbare, and even the uniforms of the moody-looking staff were old and grey. The high-domed ceiling made the great hall draughty, and the boy stood shivering while he waited for somebody to come and fetch him.

Joey didn't know what was awaiting him. He felt mildly anxious. From what he'd already seen, it would be a long, gloomy stay. After what seemed like an hour, a bossy woman arrived. She had grey hair and a long, thin, drawn face. She looked as miserable as the room that he was standing in. Joey thought she looked like a corpse that had risen from the dead.

Joey greeted her in a friendly manner. Unfortunately, his friendliness was met with a sneer. She didn't introduce herself or explain the next step of the admissions procedure.

"Walk," she ordered him as if he were a docile, knackered old cart horse.

A young woman joined them. In comparison, she seemed friendly, and she even smiled at Joey. She raised her finger to her lips, indicating for him to be quiet. It was evident that the young woman was afraid of the harridan that they were following

The boy was led down endless long grey corridors. Whenever they encountered another inmate, nobody said a word. Finally, after a long walk through the maze of grey passageways, they reached their destination. Joey presumed that they were at the back of the building. The bossy lady opened a black door and pushed him inside. He was told to wait.

The young woman stayed with Joey. She looked at the poor lad. Although she had lost her father to tuberculosis, her mother was still fighting fit. The thought of being an orphan at his tender age broke her heart.

"What is that lady's name?" asked Joey.

"The cheerful one? Mrs Jolly." answered the young nurse with a wink.

Joey began to laugh but stifled the sound. The nurse started to laugh too.

"Jolly? Really?" asked Joey.

"No, I'm joking. Her name's Mrs Grey."

Joey frowned mischievously.

"Are you pulling my leg again?"

"Tsch. Would I lie to you, young man?"

They doubled up with silent laughter, putting their hands in front of their mouths to stifle their guffaws.

"Really? That grey old woman is called 'Mrs Grey'?"

"Yes, really. That's the truth, I swear."

Joey felt better knowing he'd made a friend in this godforsaken place.

A short while later, Mrs Grey returned with a set of clothing for the boy. Everything was grey except for a brown pullover. He wasn't expecting much, but the fabric was cold and coarse.

"Follow me," Grey ordered.

Joey walked behind her, alongside the nurse, to the end of a wide corridor.

"Before putting those new clothes on, you need a good scrub. Nurse Anderson will make sure you follow the rules."

"Pleased to meet you, Nurse Anderson," Joey bowed.

"Mary," she whispered.

The nurse showed him into a bare room that stank of carbolic soap. In the middle, a man stood next to a large galvanised bathtub.

"This is Mr Jefferson."

The water was like a thick black soup. It looked as if a group of chimney sweeps had washed in it. Joey looked at the gloop and pulled up his nose. The man on duty wasn't impressed by Joey's attitude, and he gave the new boy a smack across the back of the head.

"Get undressed. Now."

Joey complied, his scalp still stinging from the clout.

"Where do you come from then?" asked the man.

"Straight out of Dorset Street, sir."

"Whitechapel then?"

It was more a statement than a question.

"Aye, sir."

"I bet you have never seen a tub of water in your life. Get in there and take that look off your face."

"It looks as if you've had a dozen coal miners through there, sir."

"Get that bloody ridiculous hat off your head."

"I prefer it on, sir."

"I don't care. I said remove it," Jefferson growled in his face. "What is your name, boy?"

"Joey Tophat."

He smiled broadly while his teeth chattered and offered a shaky hand.

"I know you, lad. I took a lot of money off you."

"How so?" Joey asked.

"It was a Friday afternoon. I bet on every race at Newmarket. I played every race until I spent all my wages. Kept thinking I could win back my losses. The old lady would have been furious. I was already in hoc to Fischer, that Jew in Spitalfields. Couldn't get by without him. Gambling debts and a few pints too many, a woman here and there. It all adds up. The good thing was I won most of my money back in the last race. Picked a real outsider I did, and it went and won by a nose. Took Eliza O'Shea's money right off her, so I did. Right cleaned her out. Good-looking wench she is, too, if I remember."

He put his head back and roared with laughter.

"I broke the bank, so I did. Lady Luck smiled on me that day."

"I am glad that I made you happy, Mr Jefferson."

'I'll make sure your luck runs out soon, though,' thought Joey.

The water wasn't only dirty, but it was also cold. He took the bar of carbolic soap and was made to scrub himself from head to toe. He finished and climbed out of the bath, shivering and shaking. All he wanted was to get dressed.

"I'm not done with you, boy," barked Mr Jefferson.

Mr Jefferson grabbed him by the arm. Joey saw a cutthroat razor in his other hand.

"You all have lice," Mr Jefferson said as he began shaving Joey's head. "Careful now. If you move, I may be tempted to nick your ear—or your throat."

At least Mr Jefferson was enjoying himself.

When Jefferson was finished, he threw some blue powder on Joey's head. Big clouds of it hung in the air. It stuck in Joey's throat, and he began to choke. Mr Jefferson stood back, looked at his handiwork and laughed. Joey touched his stubbly head and laughed even louder than Jefferson. Joey's insolent attitude irritated Jefferson, and his dislike for the boy grew. He slapped Joey firmly against his blue scalp and gave him such a shove the lad lost his footing. The boy knew a bully when he met one and would make sure that Mr Jefferson would never get another loan out of Raffi Fischer or any other money lender in the East End.

"This will be your uniform while you stay here," Nurse Mary Anderson told him. "You will wear these at all times, and we will wash them once a week. Put them on and give me your old clothes."

"We will either give them to poorer people than you or burn them," added Jefferson as he strode out of the room.

Nurse Anderson bent over and tried to take Joey's top hat and coat, but he grabbed them away from her and stamped his foot.

"That is the only hat I have," Joey told her, "and I am not giving it to you."

Nurse Anderson was surprised by Joey's stubbornness. So far, he had been cooperative.

"I got this hat and the tailcoat from my grandad. It's the only gift I have ever been given."

Joey thought a little white lie couldn't be a sin.

"Now, now, Joey," said Anderson, "we will not fight over some old clothes, will we?"

Joey's face told her he wasn't about to give in to workhouse protocol. A struggle ensued.

"Alright. If these mean that much to you, I'll put them somewhere safe—as long as you don't tell anyone."

"Thank you!" whispered Joey sincerely, grateful his beaming little face still had the power to endear.

"I'll take good care of your things until you leave," she vowed, "although you may outgrow them by the age of seventeen."

Joey nodded his blue head reluctantly, then passed the hat and coat to the smiling nurse.

"I am not living here until I am seventeen," the lad stated firmly.

Nurse Anderson gave him a weak smile as she held his hat and coat as if they were the crown jewels. Not a wealthy woman, she, too, understood how simple items could become especially important to people who had nothing.

Joey slipped into his inmate's uniform. It fitted him as badly as he expected and felt as awful as it looked. It made him fidget as he tugged the scratchy fabric away from his soft skin.

"Ready to go to your ward?"

Joey nodded again. Another white lie. He trudged behind Nurse Anderson as she paced along another long corridor.

"I live in that dormitory over there," she told Joey as she pointed out a large room, complete with twelve beds.

She looked around furtively to make sure they were alone.

"You see that bed right on the end under the window? And that tall green cupboard standing next to it? Your belongings will be in there."

Joey dipped his head in solemn agreement, knowing that he didn't have much choice in the matter, and he also appreciated that she was making a great effort to keep him happy. However, he couldn't see the governor being happy with their arrangement if it was discovered.

"What's it really like in here?" Joey asked.

Nurse Anderson gave him a side glance with a weak smile.

"Keep your head down and try not to get into any trouble, and you'll be alright."

Joey understood what that meant. It wasn't the answer he was hoping for, but the one he was expecting.

Since he'd arrived, he'd only heard three voices. Nurse Anderson, Mr Jefferson, and the corpse lady.

Even in horrid old Dorset Street, there had always been laughter. This building was as eerie as a cemetery.

9

THE NEPHEW

The letter lay on Frank Lawrence's desk in London for two weeks before he opened it. It was just as well he'd arrived in London the day before. That correspondence would have laid on his desk for a month, which would have been a disaster.

Frank opened the envelope and sighed. Everything always seemed to happen at once.

Lawrence seldom used his valet as a messenger, but this was an emergency. His pen nib scratched along a fresh sheet of ivory paper as he outlined the situation. Then, he had it delivered to Clarice's apartment.

*

Martha Lawrence sat in the corner of the study, looking as miserable as ever. Frank was behind his desk, wearing a worried expression. Clarice sat opposite her father and read the initial letter aloud.

Dear Mr Lawrence

After some extensive research, our records show that you are the brother of Mrs Darlene Cornish of Dorset Street, Whitechapel. Mrs Cornish noted you as her next of kin.

Mrs Cornish is the late mother of Joseph Charles Cornish.

He is now in the custody of Her Majesty, Queen Victoria at Slate House Workhouse, in the orphanage wing. If you do not have the means to support him, he will reside at this institution until the age of eleven. He will then be transferred to the Allan Street Workhouse in St Pancras, from which he will be released when he turns seventeen.

Yours sincerely,

Mr Edwin Hetherington

Head of Juvenile Care Provision (Spitalfields), London Metropolitan Borough

*

Softly, Clarice placed the note back on the desk.

"Since when did you have a sister, Frank?" barked Martha.

"We went our separate ways years ago," snapped Frank. "We lost touch when I left for

America. The last I heard, she started hanging around with the wrong crowd. To be honest, I thought she was dead."

"This is absurd!" Martha whined.

"You know full well that I have siblings. You seem to have lost your memory since arriving in London," snapped a sarcastic Frank.

"I have a disgrace for a husband. Clarice is a disaster. Now, there is this ragged little workhouse brat who needs care."

As usual, Martha was cold and cruel, thinking of no one but herself.

"Darlene was a spirited girl," Frank admitted. "She couldn't imagine being forced to stay on a farm for the rest of her life. We were an ordinary family, and she saw herself as more."

"She was ridiculous to think she could escape her fate," Martha observed critically.

"She was just like you, Martha. You were the daughter of a factory owner. You have washed floors and packed shelves as a child. You were no better than Darlene."

Martha knew that what Frank said was true. She'd erased those dreadful early years from her mind and created a new reality for herself. It was precisely what

Darlene had done, except Martha had fared a little better.

"I have more respect for Darlene than I have for you, wife."

Martha turned bright red.

"How dare you say that to me, Frank!"

Snorting with rage, he slammed the desk with both fists.

"You lacked the courage to come to London and seek your own fortune. At least Darlene didn't ride on the coattails of someone else. You only pursued me because you knew about my time in America. As soon as we were married, you began your silly pursuit of fame. When I received the ridiculous knighthood, to silence me, you began with your demands. You have everything you need to live a happy life. Perhaps I should give you more so I never have to see you again?"

Clarice couldn't believe that her gentle father was capable of such anger. She'd never witnessed him attack her mother in such a manner. But Frank had spent years quietly tolerating his selfish wife. Now, years of pent-up anger exploded from him.

"Can't the father look after the boy? Why you?"

"I doubt anyone knows who the father is. The last I heard, she ended up in Whitechapel. He's probably dead too. Can you remember the tour you took through the East End? You took immense pleasure in gloating at the poor and destitute. I can imagine your nose turned up at the stink of that filthy hell hole. Then you came back here to your respectable house and had a tea party with your friends."

"Those people are not humans. Rats are cleaner."

"If you ever say that again, I will sell this house. Let's see how you cope when your comfort blanket is wrenched away from you. I will give every penny I earn from the proceeds to a charity that helps those poor people."

"You will make a fool of yourself if you do that," Martha countered.

"No. I will make a fool of you, Martha. I am happy with my life away from the capital with my sheep and cows for company. It's you who wants a lavish lifestyle, not me."

Martha sniffed. Her nose was still out of joint after the confrontation, but she knew she needed to be cautious. She'd underestimated her husband, viewing him as pliable, subservient. That had changed now he had bared his teeth.

"Surely, we can attempt to trace the boy's father?"

"I doubt that. Once Darlene found her way to Whitechapel, I expect she worked as a prostitute."

"What?" Martha gasped.

"A prostitute. I am sure you know what a prostitute is."

Martha couldn't suppress her reaction.

"This is an outrage!"

"You have no choice but to accept it, my dear," he yelled.

"Keep your tone down," she ordered Frank. "Every servant in this house can hear you. This conversation will be around London by dinner time. We are barely recovering after Clarice disgraced us."

The girl glared at her mother and then spoke.

"But the boy's name is Cornish, father, not Lawrence. So, she must have married, no?"

"Anyone can change their name in Whitechapel. No one checks—or cares. So, it's likely that she never had a husband, and the father was an absent one at best. Chances are he doesn't even know."

The letter had shaken Frank to the core. He wasn't surprised by the death of his wayward sister. Darlene had never been responsible. But to learn that she was the mother of a living, breathing eight-year-old was a shock.

"What are you going to do, father?"

"He is family, Clarice, and we will raise him as such."

"Don't you dare bring an illegitimate child into this house and expect me to raise him," spat Martha.

"You couldn't raise your own child, Martha, so why would I ask you to look after this boy? He can come and live on the farm with me. Or, I will find a governess, and we will get on with the job of raising him here."

"As long as you portray him as a servant, it should not affect—"

Martha didn't have time to finish the sentence.

"—This is my house. I own it. If I tell you that the boy will live here, then he will. Now, get out of my study. I don't want to see you for the rest of the day. Or perhaps longer."

Martha burst into a flood of tears. Ordinarily mild-mannered, Frank had never treated her in this way before, and she was afraid. She didn't want to lose her magnificent London house, and she certainly didn't relish being a disgraced divorcee on the peripheries of society. Now meek and sulking, she left the study to lick her wounds and consider how to salvage her future. Frank stood up and slammed the door behind her.

Dark and brooding, Frank Lawrence didn't want to talk to anyone, not even Clarice. He could only manage a few instructions.

"I am sailing to New York in the morning. I have some business to attend to," he said, pushing the letter towards her. "Will you take care of this?"

Clarice nodded and then folded the note back into its envelope as her father jotted down another memo.

"Find Master Joseph. Consult the authorities on my behalf. Here, take this note."

He passed her the paper.

"It confirms you are my proxy. My solicitor Mr Stanton will help you if needs be."

She bent down and kissed her father on the cheek. Then, she took both notes and slipped them discreetly into her pocket.

"I love you, Papa. Please don't worry about anything while you are away. I will do my best for you—and the boy."

10

THE ESCAPE

"They have very strict rules here," Nurse Anderson told Joey.

"You are not allowed to make a noise. You are not allowed to waste food. You wake up at five o'clock. You eat breakfast at six. Then you start work. Your day ends at seven. You must be in bed, asleep, by ten. There is a meagre iron stove in the corner where you will sleep."

"Where will I work? Here?" asked Joey.

"Yes. Orphans normally work onsite, in the grounds, but in some cases, people will come here and hire you for labour."

"Oh good," said Joey enthusiastically, "I love being outside—and working! I hate being idle."

"I don't think you understand, Joey. Most of the work they require you to do is terrible."

"What do you mean by that?"

"Emptying the slops—"

Her voice trailed off.

"I've done that before," Joey chirped with a smile. "The world didn't end."

Mary Anderson gave a delighted laugh, and it echoed down the corridor. She was the only person that Joey would see smile for the rest of his stay. Everybody else was miserable.

The nurse took him up to the draughty loft where at least sixty boys of various ages slept. Two masters saw to it that everybody behaved themselves. As reality struck, Joey froze. Nurse Anderson pushed him through the door and then left him there.

At first, he thought he heard the cries of an injured dog. Then he realised that a brutish master had given a five-year-old little boy a severe caning. The little boy tried to wriggle from the man's grasp on his collar to escape another thrashing.

Joey couldn't bear the sight of it. An older boy saw Joey heave, and he put his fingers to his lips.

"Shhh. Or you'll be next."

Joey wanted to cry. He'd never seen such cruelty.

"What did he do?" Joey whispered to a nearby inmate.

"He spilt his tea at the breakfast table this morning."

"That was all?"

The boy's eyes warned Joey to shut up.

The cane thwacked against the poor boy's skin again and again. The master grunted with the effort.

"You will not—" *Thwack!* "Do that again!" *Thwack!* "Understand?"

The boy sobbed uncontrollably as blood seeped through his clothing.

"Shut up!" *Thwack!*

The master cupped his hand over the boy's mouth and nose and left it there until the lad's eyes blinked and bulged out like a toad's. Next, the brute shoved the child to the floor, followed by his heavy hobnailed boot kicking him in the belly.

"Be more careful in future. Is that clear?" bellowed the master. "Is it? Answer me, boy."

Frozen with contempt, Joey said nothing. He'd lived in the worst part of the city, and he'd never lived through such a horrible event.

The monster eventually relented and left the attic, sweat dripping from his brow. When the man was gone, Joey whispered:

"What's his name?"

"Officially, Hebdon. But we call him 'The Devil Himself.'"

Joey's heart was beating ten to one, and he was terrified.

"Do you see that great big lad over there?" said the other boy. "That's Curtis Harrison. He has lived here since he was a babe in arms. He has seen a lot. Curtis has vowed to have both of Hebdon's legs broken when he is let out next month. Curtis says he won't do it himself, but he swears that Hebdon will never walk again."

Joey thought it best not to get on the wrong side of Curtis Harrison either.

"I'm Alfie Jones," said the lad, offering a hearty handshake. "You are?"

"Joey. Do we go to school for lessons?" he asked, trying to take his mind off the horror he found himself in.

"What do you think this is, mate? A holiday?"

Alfie sounded about 20 years older than he was.

"We are here to work. On Sunday, we have two hours of school. Sometimes we get to see a book. Not often, mind."

Joey nodded as Alfie shrugged.

"I don't mind that at all," Alfie said, not blessed with Joey's aptitude to learn. "It would be better if they left us alone to sit around here for two hours on a Sunday."

"You have to learn to read and write," Joey told him seriously.

"What for?"

"How long have you been here?" Joey asked Alfie.

"Let's see. I was seven," answered Alfie. "Now, I am going on eleven, so that's, err—"

Alfie looked blank and began counting on his fingers.

"Four years," added Joey with a smile. "What do you do all day?"

"We mostly clean," muttered Alfie. "We clean the privies and the kitchens. Then there are the stables. We take the horse muck down to the allotment. Some boys work on the plots down there. We reckon it's the best place because you're outdoors all day. We can smoke, and they leave us alone mostly."

Joey's mind was moving at a rapid pace.

"How do I get to work in the garden?"

"Oh, that depends. The older boys get the jobs outside because the wee lads aren't strong

enough to graft all day. Mr Atkins usually
picks older lads who can push a barrow.
Atkins is a decent sort. Relatively speaking,
like. Everyone wants to work with him. Bit of
a soft touch."

Joey nodded. The little whippersnapper who had
received the beating had stopped screaming now and
was being comforted by older boys. Although the lads in
the workhouse could display frightful cruelty towards
one another, they were unanimous in their hatred of
Hebdon. The smell of rebellion permeated the air. The
continual beatings had amalgamated them as one.

Many of the boys had suffered the cruelty of these
monsters for many years. Pacts were constantly being
made between the youngsters. When they were older,
more importantly, free, they all secretly wanted to find
their tormentors and persecute them.

Joey's sense of humour suddenly got the better of him.
The threats must have been real because the obituary
columns were full of names of honoured government
employees who had met their deaths in unusual ways.
Joey remembered a story of a headmaster who had
suffered a heart attack. The curious thing was his corpse
was found in the storeroom where he kept a collection
of canes. The canes were polished to perfection. The
accompanying photograph gave the impression that the
room was better suited to the private torture of pupils
than storage.

*

At night, the large orphan dormitory was cold. The wood-burning stove was desperately inadequate. It barely added even a degree of warmth to the cavernous architecture. Any boy who dared complain that he was cold was punished and made to sleep on the cold floor for the rest of the night. Each child slept on a cot adorned with a worn-out mattress and one scratchy grey blanket. There was no such thing as a pillow to rest their weary heads on. Most of the boys had grown up in such poverty and were used to trying conditions. The lack of sufficient bedclothes mattered not. The iciness in the room was horrid, but that of the staff was worse, and no amount of bedding could protect them from that.

Joey pondered his circumstances. The people in Dorset Street were drunks, prostitutes, criminals, even murderers. But even in such dire straits, people still laughed and gave a wry smile. There were no such variables in the orphanage. The only person who was known to be kind was Miss Anderson. There was a lot of gossip that Nurse Anderson would get the sack soon because she was too kind. She simply didn't have the heart to enforce the harsh discipline expected of her. When no one was looking, her compassion always shone through.

The rest of the staff displayed no acts of kindness, or any empathy. Some children were suffering from cholera or TB. They were separated from the general inmate population and moved to the basement, where the conditions were deplorable. The only inlet for air and light was a tiny window in the shape of a half-moon that peeped out above the damp earth. Although the window was high up on the wall, out of the children's reach, it still had thick iron bars guarding it. Damp permeated the walls. The Board of Guardians justified the poor facilities by saying that the room was adequately aired for those with respiratory diseases, and the conditions ensured a speedy recovery. They turned a blind eye to the moss and mildew that grew against the walls. It was far easier to just give the place a good clean in the days preceding a visit by the government's medical officer. Very few patients recovered, but nobody cared.

"What happens if you try to run away, Alfie?"

"Well, that is a serious crime. Usually, they take the fella to the magistrate."

"And the sentence?"

"Ha. Surely you know that everything in Britain is solved with a jolly good whipping these days. They flay you until you are too terrified to ever try it again."

Joey's rage was replacing his fear.

"They take us to the police station. Every station has got a constable who is appointed to the job. Our constabulary has an Irish chap. A right ogre, he is. The name's Murphy. More like 'monster'," cursed Alfie, his eyes full of hatred. "He will beat the skin off your back without blinking an eye."

Joey was repulsed by the thought of ending up in a police station with a brute of an Irishman. Just hearing of these ordeals was terrifying. He thought his life had been challenging at times before, but this was something else altogether. The idea of living in a place like this until he was seventeen was soul-crushing. It was a gaol in all but name. For Joey, the real pity was that the children were separated from their parents—and bad things seemed to happen when there were no adults to protect them. There was clearly only one option for Joey Tophat—escape. Else he would surely face the wrath of the Irishman sooner or later.

*

Joey spent his time studying the people and the building, the comings and goings, the openings, entrances and exits.

Finally, he saw a weakness in the management of the inmates—and he was determined to take advantage of it. Soon his plan was in full swing.

As always, he displayed a cheerful disposition, albeit forced. Mr Atkins liked his pleasant and polite demeanour, so it was easy to be chosen to work in the garden most days.

In Joey's mind's eye, the first step was complete.

The wily lad used the opportunity to scour the workhouse perimeter and identified the most difficult spot to breach the wall. Why there? Because he reasoned that the board would expect any sensible escapee to use the easiest route. Joey Tophat never saw himself as 'predictable'.

Every Friday night, the boys had to bathe in the filthy admissions chamber under the supervision of Mr Jefferson, who took great pleasure in staring at the long line of naked boys. As the boys finished washing, they were marched back to the dormitory. Sometimes, the boys were escorted back to their loft by Jefferson too. Each time, the brute found a reason to pick on Harry Smith, a puny twelve-year-old. He would order the boy out of the line, saying he would be taken off somewhere for punishment. Then he would order the column of lads back to the dormitory alone. Later, Harry would return quiet, withdrawn, and sad. The depraved reason for Jefferson singling him out was all too apparent, even to the younger lads.

Joey knew that he would use this opportunity to slip from the column. He also knew that nobody would snitch.

Joey did everything that was expected of him. On the one hand, he did them well because that was his nature. A hard worker, doing his best always gave him a sense of pride. On the other, he had his secret agenda to manage.

During his short stay in the orphanage wing, Joey became a favourite overnight. The staff had never met a boy who was so obedient and happy to follow all the instructions that he was given. He didn't fight with the other children. He didn't bully the little ones. Years in the company of adults equipped him to fend them off. Joey had accomplished precisely what he'd set out to do in step two. He had lulled the staff into a false sense of security, and within seven days, they became complacent. It was time for Joey to wait patiently for one last Friday night bathe.

*

He climbed out of the dirty tub, noticing a layer of dirt caked on, the residue from the other boys who had washed before him. He dressed in the fresh nightclothes issued to him and fell into line.

Jefferson ordered them to walk and gave Joey no trouble at all. In fact, that night, he gave Joey an eerily friendly greeting, which sent shivers down the boy's spine. The orphans marched in single file towards their dormitory. Regular as clockwork, Jefferson isolated Harry and ordered the rest to continue. Then, with the tormentor's back turned, Joey struck. He slipped out of line and darted off in the opposite direction, silently disappearing into the gloom. The other boys looked on agog, but none uttered a sound.

Joey had only been in the east wing of the building once and was afraid that he would get lost. The staff supper time coincided perfectly with the bathing roster. While Mary Anderson ate her dinner, she'd no clue that Joey had embarked on his escape.

Joey went to her bed, tiptoed around it, and opened the large green wardrobe. As he swung open the door, his face lit up. On the top shelf was his beloved top hat, resting on his coat. He was glad that he'd insisted she should keep it. The weather was freezing outside.

He didn't change clothes in the room. That was far too much of a risk. Instead, he climbed on another staff wardrobe and slithered his lithe little body through the narrow window above, Civvy Street clothes in hand.

Clamping his jaw to silence his chattering teeth, Joey hid in the shadows and dressed, then ran down the long driveway towards the imposing front gates of the institution. He'd decided to scale the large cast-iron gates that lead to the storage warehouses.

Joey found a tree close to the gates and climbed it. The journey from the tree's overhanging limb to the top of the gate was risky. Joey took a tremendous jump, landed on the top of the gate with an almighty clang, wobbled, then lost his balance and fell back onto the driveway. He limped off back to the shadows as a guard dog barked in the distance, and the crunch of footsteps on the flagstones filled the air. Alone and afraid, Joey's heart threatened to bang out of his chest. Two guards peered out into the yard, their eyes straining in the dark.

"It's nothing, Bill. Come on, let's finish our card game. It's nippy out tonight."

"Ready to lose, again, are ya?"

"Oi!"

The two men retreated to their warm office.

Joey climbed the tree again, and this time he had better luck. He over compensated, and his momentum sent him flying over the gate. Falling eight feet, he thudded to the ground, winded—but free. Even if he'd broken his leg, Joey Tophat would have dragged himself away. Thankfully nothing was broken, and soon he was dashing about looking for a hiding place.

The good news was he'd escaped. The bad news was he was still in a predicament.

He couldn't go back to Dorset Street. It was the first place the authorities would look for him. He couldn't go back to Eliza. That would get her into a lot of trouble. He couldn't approach Raffi Fischer, Joey didn't know the man well enough, and their first encounter had been 'frosty', to say the least. He'd burned his bridges with Mr and Mrs Chang long ago.

The second clang of the gate had convinced the guards something was amiss. Shouts and the sound of footsteps filled the crisp night air. He saw the flickers of lanterns inside the grounds he'd just fled from.

At least he wasn't in his inmate's uniform. Nobody would recognise him in the tailcoat and top hat. He convinced himself he should get going. It was the first time in years that he didn't quite know what he would do next, but he kept running, knowing that safety would lie far from the workhouse.

*

Joey felt like he'd run for hours, and by the time he stopped, he was panting like a racehorse, white air steaming from his mouth and nostrils. About him, he saw that the whole city had changed. He was no longer in the East End but the West End, surrounded by stately buildings. Feeling safer, he walked on. Finally, he turned into a vaguely familiar street. He recognised the British Museum immediately. It was where he and Eliza had spent a few wonderful days together.

Joey couldn't say why he did it, but he climbed over the wall to the museum. Perhaps he was attracted to it because he'd experienced happiness there. He kept to the shadows, hidden in the dark. The British Museum was colossal. No lights shone from the windows. Judging by the last time he heard a bell toll, he estimated the time to be approximately 10 o'clock. He snuck around the back of the museum, not knowing what he was doing there. The building was attracting him like a magnet would summon an iron bar.

Joey passed a small enclave and stopped to peep into it. He was surprised when he stumbled upon a door—an open door. A dull but welcoming yellow lamp glowed inside. Joey crept towards the heavy door. He peered in and found himself staring into a great room. The beauty of the room took his breath away. It was lined with large murals and displays. He'd been in the room before with Eliza. His interest was piqued in an instant.

Joey put his head through the door frame and looked around him. He wondered if somebody had forgotten to lock the door for the night. How stupid, he thought. Everything inside was priceless. Joey was about five paces into the room when he heard footsteps growing louder. Joey darted behind a display case and prayed that he could become invisible. The man passed by the cabinet. He was tall and thin and wore a bowler hat. It was all that Joey could make out. He heard the man rattle some keys.

The heavy door creaked as Mr Featherstone moved it. Then there was a thunderous crash as the door closed, reverberating throughout the building. The key turned in the lock. Young Joey Tophat was trapped inside again.

11

THE COFFEE HOUSE IN CHELSEA

Thomas McGill shook the London rain from his umbrella. He stepped into the doorway of the coffee house, which went by the name of 'The Great Coffee Emporium.' It was situated in an avant-garde area of Chelsea.

His regular haunt was the 'The Cigar Lounge' in Mayfair. He loved being recognised as a patron of such a renowned establishment. The owner was a canny one. Most coffee houses were advertised as cigar shops because they attracted the two types of clientele. Elegant rosewood shelves were lined with exotic smokes from the Americas and some less exotic ones made in the East End. Ragged street urchins lurked in the shadows, waiting to pick up discarded butts as the patrons left. If they collected a hundred or so, they could raise a tidy sum by selling them back to a middle man who often took them to the local cigar factories.

Thomas McGill knew it was fashionable to be seen at the venue and spent a lot of time poring over the vast selection of tobacco flavours. He would choose a cigar with a flourish that said, 'I am experienced.' This was a lie. Everything that Thomas did was a sham.

He enjoyed the elegance and culture of the upmarket venue. The patrons were the more cerebral sorts who radiated a sombre intelligence. Russian ex-pats sat in the shadows where they played chess or practised the game alone. Being associated with intellectual sorts made Thomas feel successful. He displayed his pride by puffing out his chest and making loud requests to get attention. He tried to shake off his reputation of being a dandy.

There was no entry fee to 'The Great Coffee Emporium', which was unusual. Usually, he paid a shilling which earned him a cup of coffee and a cigar. He was perplexed the moment he entered the room. The ambience was dissimilar to what he experienced in the upmarket suburbs of London. The atmosphere was almost revolutionary. Loud, opinionated, aggressive, and wrought with political contempt for his class.

Thomas had gone to great lengths to identify Clarice Lawrence's regular retreats, and he'd been informed that she frequented this coffee house in particular. He put aside his disdain for the patrons to concentrate on his reason for being there. Thomas had every intention of seducing Clarice into marriage. She came from money. She was educated. He would never become bored with a spirited creature like Clarice. Agreed, she didn't meet her mother's exacting standards, but he suspected few ladies ever would.

The coffee house was already filled with patrons, but they were not of the quietly chattering upper classes. These people were loud and gathered there to meet the like-minded. Here they shared ideas on economics, criticised politicians, and voiced their disagreement with the arcane social mores that their queen demanded from her subjects. They conducted business, shared gossip, deliberated all topical subjects, and discussed any and all news of interest.

'The Great Coffee Emporium' served alcohol to its patrons. More significantly, they served alcohol to women. He observed that the fairer sex indulged in whisky, cognac, and vodka. The women in attendance were debating as passionately as the men. Thomas McGill felt uncomfortable. He was surrounded by Suffragettes, libertarians, and Marxists. One thing was certain, his mother had been correct about Clarice's ideological affiliations. It wasn't just her attire that was wayward. Thomas was overwhelmed with lust for Clarice Lawrence. He didn't want a wife like the archetypal caged songbird, pretty to look at but restrained and dull. A little bit of edginess had to be a good thing. He decided he could overlook any of her shortcomings, presuming she could be coaxed to grow out of most of them in time.

Thomas took the last remaining seat, a high chair by the bar counter. He had hoped for something less prominent, but there were no deep, luxurious leather sofas to relax on, only round tub chairs and stools around low tables. At the far side of the room, he spotted Clarice at a table in a corner packed with authors, poets, and artists. Thomas recognised some of them. He couldn't wrench his eyes away from Clarice. He was bewitched. When he wasn't lounging around irritating his parents, Thomas had spent days considering how he would tame her. It was cunning and disturbing. His sole objective was to follow her home, where he would approach her alone. Then he fantasised about more until the bartender broke the spell.

"A Partagàs and a Jameson's whisky, please.
Oh, and a copy of the evening newspaper."

Thomas opened the journal, intent on looking normal even though he'd read it earlier. It also offered a convenient hiding place to observe his prey. His eyes peeped over the top of the paper. He thought about how these London coffeehouses had earned the nickname 'penny universities.' An interesting name, borne in relation to the cost of a cup of coffee and the sober debates ignited within. Historically, polite and reasoned talk touched on literature, poetry, politics, science, commerce, and religion. But this establishment was none of that. It was a subversive meeting place of radical thinkers.

The establishment thought the Temperance Movement had made a grave mistake. The cheap prices opened up the coffeehouses of the working classes. 'The Great Coffee Emporium' in Chelsea was a breeding ground for revolution. It was everything his parents abhorred.

It was close to midnight when Clarice got up to leave. Thomas knocked back the last of his whisky and followed her. Luckily, it was a busy night, making his task much more manageable. Knowing that Clarice was unaware of his presence filled him with ecstasy. She was being escorted home by a young man. When they reached the door to her lodgings, she smiled and thanked him. Thomas was delighted to see the man doff his hat and then leave.

Clarice was tired. She'd had a demanding day at the university and spent more time relaxing at the coffee house than she'd intended. As she put her coat on the stand, she heard the familiar creak of the staircase and the sound of footsteps making their way down the corridor. They became louder, then stopped right outside. She was surprised to hear a light rap on her door at such a late hour and guessed it was her neighbour, Elizabeth.

Elizabeth was also a wild and artistic type who devoted her life to painting incredible murals. She often stopped by after a night out to share the details of her latest suitor. Yawning, Clarice would pour them each a cup of tea and listen to her friend's ramblings. She dragged herself to the door, mumbling and hoping the visit would be short.

"You!" she blurted out when she saw Thomas.

His eyes scanned every inch of her body. She was barefoot and wearing a stunning gold kimono, tightly cinched in at the waist but looser around the chest, revealing her décolletage. Her hair flowed around her face, framing it perfectly, then tumbled down over her shoulders. She looked seductive, warm, and wild— everything that Thomas imagined and hoped she could be.

Clarice studied Thomas for a few seconds. She didn't utter a word. He was caught off guard by her silence, believing that he deserved a warm welcome or at least the courtesy of a greeting. Nothing.

"Hello, Clarice."

She continued to study him. Thomas began to fidget. He tried to sound confident.

"I know it is very late, but—"

Clarice didn't respond.

"—I was wondering if I can come in?"

She frowned and tilted her head to one side.

"Ah, yes," he fumbled. "I saw you at the coffeehouse around the corner, and you were so deep in conversation I didn't want to interrupt. And—"

Thomas was desperate to legitimise his reason for standing in her doorway at midnight.

"Well, uhm. I saw you leave the coffeehouse with that gentleman and I was concerned for your safety. I decided I would make sure you got home safely. You can't be too careful."

It was an incredible but believable lie. The front door of the building slammed shut, and the noise reverberated up the stairs. Whoever was arriving home was creating a commotion.

"May I come in? Briefly?" Thomas asked. "Your neighbours will not be impressed with a man standing at your door at this late hour."

Clarice was about to give Thomas his marching orders when Elizabeth appeared on the landing. Her face broke into a broad smile.

"Darling!" Elizabeth whooped as she ambushed Clarice, barging Thomas out of the way as she flung her arms around her friend.

"I am delighted that you're still awake. Gosh! I have so much to tell you," Elizabeth chortled.

"Evening, Lizzy."

She turned to Thomas and smiled at him.

"So sorry to interrupt, darling. It's just that I have had such a wonderful evening."

Thomas grinned sheepishly.

"Come on, Clarry, make us all a cup of tea, and I will tell you everything."

Before Clarice could stop her, Elizabeth took Thomas's arm and shoved him into Clarice's apartment.

*

Elizabeth's nonstop chattering alleviated the tension between Clarice and Thomas. Elizabeth went into depth over the people she'd met.

"Dear old Jeremy introduced me to a chap— from Munich of all places—who admires my paintings and said he will make me famous in Germany. A theatre owner who is friends with George Bernard Shaw said I must design the set for George's next lavish West End production."

Elizabeth didn't stop talking until Clarice had finished making the tea.

"And who are you?" she asked McGill when she eventually calmed down.

"I'm Thomas. Our mothers are friends."

Thomas was taken aback by the wild, outrageous woman. Elizabeth was underwhelmed. She studied him briefly. There was nothing impressive about him at all. *'Has Clarice lost her mind entertaining such a whimsey? Urgh.'*

"Clarry, I am meeting the German tomorrow. Please come with me. I need your educated opinion on the matter."

"I am sorry, Lizzy. I have business to take care of tomorrow."

"Business? That sounds official—and very dull and grown-up. Make an excuse. Come to the party."

"My father has had to go away on business. Before he left, he asked me to find someone."

"Who?"

"A family member who has been sent to the workhouse—"

"—what?" interrupted Thomas on hearing another thing about Clarice that would disappoint his mother.

"My young cousin has been admitted into the local workhouse orphanage, and I need to fetch him."

Thomas was confused. He'd been led to believe that Clarice came from a fine family, or it certainly looked that way. Now, it had come to light that she had a cousin in the workhouse. His future with Clarice was looking bleaker by the moment.

"The boy's mother died. My father's estranged sister. She listed Papa as the lad's next of kin. Obviously, we will have to take him in. Mother is livid, of course."

"Where did he live until he became an orphan? Near the family farm?" asked Thomas.

"No. Dorset Street," replied Clarice.

Elizabeth's eyes widened. Thomas looked pale. It didn't sound like a Mayfair address.

"The infamous Dorset Street? Where poor Mary Kelly—" Elizabeth shook her head in wonderment.

"Yes," answered Clarice, "that infamous Dorset Street."

"Imagine that," exclaimed Elizabeth. "Perhaps he can give us some information on the murderer."

It dawned on Thomas why the place rang a bell: '*The Ripper!*' This new development was guaranteed to make his mother apoplectic. Yet, while the whole situation confounded him, he was an opportunist.

"I will escort you to the workhouse, Clarice. It sounds like official business. You will need male accompaniment for protection. And since your father is away—"

"I agree with you, Thomas. You will need help tomorrow, Clarry."

"I'll be fine. I am only visiting, and I have a letter from papa. They are not going to admit me, for goodness' sake."

Elizabeth raised her eyebrows, and a patronising Thomas tutted at her supposed foolhardiness.

"Elizabeth is right, Clarice, I insist."

"Thank you, Thomas. That's settled then. You're so lucky to have a friend like this fine young fellow."

Sighing, Clarice surrendered. It was the only way she could get rid of them for the night.

*

As Thomas sauntered home, he lamented that he would never be allowed to marry Clarice. This new development in the Lawrence family would be viewed as scandalous. Dorset Street. The Ripper. Workhouses. Orphans. Faced with so many obstacles, it wasn't a battle he could ever win. Titled or not, the Lawrence family was common. He opted to take his father's advice: seduce Clarice but don't marry her.

12

ALONE IN THE DARKNESS

Joey couldn't believe how lucky he was. He had the whole museum to himself. He also realised how stupid he'd been to get locked in. There were watchmen on duty, but spotting where they patrolled was easy. The guards swung their lamps as they walked through the corridors and the bouncing yellow glow warned of their proximity. Joey could have spent a week in the museum, and none of the men would have known he was there.

Back in their staff room, the guards tended to sit at a table eating and playing a card game. Some others had been placed in more remote parts of the building, opening up the opportunity to sleep on the job. In the dead of night, with their custodian boss safely tucked up in bed, they patrolled on foot as little as possible.

Although it was dark, Joey was fascinated by the grand building. Since his escape, Joey had been too distracted by his surroundings to consider the hour. He'd only become aware of the time when he entered a hall that displayed a great clock. He was staggered to see it was almost six in the morning. The guards seemed to become more active. A few of them referred to their shift change. Joey tried to find an exit he could slip out of later. There were many doors that the public could leave and enter, but they were all locked. Joey realised that he was trapped for the time being. If anybody found him in the British Museum at daybreak, he would be arrested and sent off to the closest constabulary. With a shudder, he remembered what Alfie had told him about Murphy, the mad Irishman with a penchant for flaying offenders.

Joey began to panic. He heard more doors open and close. There were more voices, and more laughter wafted through the air. The watchmen were changing shifts. Now, it felt like the museum was crawling with them. In fits and starts, he darted from corridor to corridor and room to room, trying to find an escape, but there was none. He considered climbing out of a window but to no avail. They were all bolted shut. So, since a second lucky escape wasn't an option, Joey Tophat plumped for concealment.

The question was, where?

Thankfully, it seemed Joey's canny knack of falling on his feet was returning. He stumbled upon a fine Jacobean furniture display. A canopy bed dominated the far end, nearly as large as the room he shared with his mother in Whitechapel. The lower part of the bed frame was solid oak, which felt smooth and cool to the touch. Its wooden posts were covered with the most intricate carving work that Joey had ever seen. It was spectacular. High above the great canopy was solid rosewood lined with gold and red striped silk. The oak headboard displayed a Flemish tapestry. The beautiful pastoral scene was so fine that he couldn't make out the individual stitches. At the corners were great curtains embroidered with the finest silk. The design teemed with pretty flowers. Lush leafy tendrils rolled and folded their way around the exquisite blossoms. Joey decided whoever designed it was a master craftsman.

His examination of the piece was halted by a fortuitous flashback. He remembered something that Eliza had told him. During the Middle Ages, fathers had made space under these huge beds for their daughters to sleep—or hide—in, protecting them from unwanted suitors or raiding soldiers.

Could this bed have such a device fitted? There was no time to lose as Joey heard footsteps coming towards him. He watched the swinging yellow glows get brighter as the watchmen got closer.

He went closer and felt around until he found heavy iron handles on the side of the bed. He grinned with relief. *'Once again, Joey Tophat has fallen on his feet.'*

He pulled at the handles, and a side panel flopped open. Slowly, silently, he lowered the door and peeped in. It was pitch dark. He had no idea what was inside, but there seemed to be quite a bit of room when he waved his arm in the newly-revealed space. He shoved his top hat in first, then scrambled into the compartment. The bed creaked, and the door thumped as he struggled to pull it to from the inside, but the watchmen saw and heard nothing, too preoccupied discussing the likely winner of a cricket match at The Oval next week.

Joey waved his hand above him, terrified his head might bang into the frame. The space was larger than it looked from the outside, and if he crouched over a bit, he could sit. It was uncomfortable, but it was safe. After the sun rose, light streamed through tiny little holes. Joey imagined that he was stargazing as he studied the pattern. They were designed to appear decorative on the outside. Joey realised they were not there to look pretty, but they were breathing holes for their young ladies who had to sleep there.

He crept onto his knees and peered through them. There had already been an influx of visitors. A room guardian sat on a chair in the corner and devoured a sandwich when he thought no one was looking. Joey realised that he'd not eaten since he escaped the workhouse. His stomach growled. He'd had no sleep, and sitting still was starting to ache. He had to make peace with the idea that he couldn't climb out of his hiding place until late that night. Joey didn't have a lot of time to ponder his dilemma. He was suddenly overcome with exhaustion, brought on by high adventure and lack of sleep, and a light doze soon became a deep slumber.

He guessed he must have slept for around ten to twelve hours because it was dark again when he woke up, and the museum was deathly quiet. He slipped out from under the bed, thirst and hunger raging. Joey had to find something to sustain him soon, or he would collapse.

He crept from the room and made his way to the area where he had seen a 'staff only' sign the night before. He tried the door and was delighted to find it was open. It led to an office that held at least thirty desks. He rifled through all the drawers, but all he found was a small packet of humbugs. He chomped on the sweets, his molars crushing them to dust in seconds. Once all the sweets were wolfed down, he returned the empty packet to the drawer.

Joey left the office and returned to the corridor. He opened another door. This time, he struck gold. He was standing in the visitor's restaurant. Now, all Joey had to do was find the kitchen where they made the food. He couldn't see an obvious door leading from the dining room to the kitchen. He investigated a little closer, and shortly, he discovered one of the large wooden panels had a hinge and a seam. He pushed with all his might, and it swung open to reveal a large kitchen. His eyes scanned his new surroundings. The place looked immaculate, crammed with pots, pans, cookers and crockery—but no food.

His gaze fell on a very welcome sign: *'Pantry'*. The annexe room was well stocked with fruit and vegetables. There was also a loaf of bread, of which three-quarters had been eaten. A few tempting cakes lurked under ornate glass lids. As one hand shoved the tasty morsels into his mouth, the other hand was busy stuffing snacks for later into his pockets. He topped up an ale bottle with water. His mind wandered. It was too risky to go straight to Eliza's. He decided that would be the first place the authorities would look for him, so he planned to hide in the bed during the day and fetch more food at night until the coast was clear. He spotted one last door in the kitchen, the cold store. On the shelves were piles of glossy pork pies and platters laden with tender slices of meat. Joey helped himself to a delicious dinner, and being a gentleman, he cleaned up after himself.

Perhaps being trapped here wasn't going to be so bad after all?

13

CLARICE'S UNWANTED ESCORT

Thomas McGill sat in his cab, waiting for Clarice to exit the building. He'd arranged to be there at nine o'clock, but he couldn't help himself, so he got there with an hour to spare, just in case she tried to give him the slip.

Clarice wore a solemn expression. Her hair was pulled harshly off her face, and she wore a dull black dress. It was her attempt to blend in with the other sheep on their way to official work. Clarice knew that the head of the workhouse, Edwin Hetherington, was a conservative man who would never tolerate her liberal views. If she had to drop her standards to fulfil her father's request and save her cousin, so be it.

Thomas opened the cab door and greeted Clarice with an exaggerated flourish. The horrid dress didn't detract from her beauty. Thomas took her hand as he helped her into the coach. He felt a vibration ripple from his hand to his groin. Thomas had little practical experience with women. He'd fumbled around at a brothel once or twice, and the experience had been as dreadful as it was artificial.

His obsession with Clarice had changed. No longer viewing her as a long-term commitment but a casual conquest, his fantasies were becoming disturbing. In the past, he'd mentioned his failings at the brothel to a few friends, and they immediately indulged him with a plethora of erotic pictures. He'd never envisaged how imaginative men could become in moments of lust and boredom and was keen to try out a few of the suggestions if the opportunity presented itself.

"You look beautiful, my dear," he said as he leaned in, his hot unwelcome breath pummelling her cheek.

Thomas didn't let go of Clarice's hand, forcing her to pull it away roughly.

"Where are we going, darling?"

"The Slater Street Workhouse," she said through gritted teeth.

Thomas yelled to the driver, and the cab leapt forward.

"I suggest you allow me to talk to Hetherington, Clarice."

"I can speak for myself. If I wanted a representative, I would have had a solicitor accompany me."

"I wasn't suggesting that you are incompetent. It is just that Hetherington is well acquainted with our family. I have no doubt that he will favour me."

Clarice wished that she'd been firmer the night before. She should never have accepted his assistance.

"My dear," cooed Thomas. "You have quite a reputation in London. Hetherington will never consider releasing the young man into your care."

"What?"

"Let me say that you are lucky that I am with you—"

"—what reputation?" Clarice demanded.

"People have noticed that you have, let's call them, err, 'liberal' views. Your dress is a clear indication of your morality. Your politics are damning. I'd say that you are quite lucky I am here. I will dignify your visit."

Clarice never expected much from Thomas, but still, she was shocked by his attack on her character. She pulled down the glass window and shouted to the driver.

"Stop. I want to get out!"

The driver brought the cab to a sudden halt. She bolted out of the carriage, with McGill clambering awkwardly behind her.

"Stop, Clarice! Please, stop!"

For once, Clarice did as she was told and turned around to face him.

"I am so sorry, my dear, if I came across too harshly. I merely meant to say that I could help you. It wasn't meant to sound like an assault on your character."

"You knew exactly what you were saying."

She glared at him, furious, her eyes like slits.

"Please calm down, my darling. It was an honest mistake." Thomas said soothingly.

Clarice tried to compose herself, but her temper had risen to the surface, and she thought of Frank. What would her father expect her to do? She stepped forward and gave Thomas a good slap.

Overhearing the kerfuffle, the cab driver stifled a smile. His grin widened further still when a bright red handmark manifested itself on the odious man's face. Clarice continued to box her travelling companion's ears.

"Never refer to me as 'dear' or ' darling' again."

She stomped off, making it clear Thomas's help at the workhouse would not be welcome.

*

Clarice stood in the foyer of Slater Street Workhouse, exactly where Joey had stood a week earlier. She also observed that it was bleak and depressing. She regretted wearing the horrible black dress. It did no good to pretend to be something that she wasn't.

She didn't have to wait long for her appointment with Mr Hetherington. There was an urgency among the staff to get her in front of him as fast as possible.

"Ah, Miss Lawrence. Take a seat, my dear. There has been an unfortunate 'development'."

Clarice ignored being referred to as dear yet again, too desperate to know what had happened.

"He has run away."

"What?"

"I said that the little lout has run away. Escaped. A few boys flee from these premises, usually the most undesirable sorts. It goes to show that he is a conniving little hooligan."

Clarice raised her eyebrows at the stereotypical man.

"Yes, Miss Lawrence, a hooligan."

Mr Hetherington was a wiry little man with no sense of humour. His intentions were probably good, but he had no knowledge of the boys' cruel treatment after he went home at night.

"I feel for the boy," he continued, "I wish he had the courtesy to wait for you to arrive before he caused all this mayhem."

"Is there any clue about where he is now?"

"How should I know Miss Lawrence? I am not a psychic or a medium."

Mr Hetherington stretched out his arm and slowly turned around to face the large window.

"Look around you, Miss Lawrence. London is a large city. He could be anywhere. There is one thing that might be helpful."

"Go on."

"Do you know that your cousin also goes under the alias, 'Joey Tophat'?"

"But his birth name is Cornish," said Clarice, confused.

"Yes, that is correct," sighed Mr Hetherington, "but everyone in Spitalfields knows him as Joey Tophat. Despite his tender age, he is a highly successful bookmaker. He and his partner, Eliza O'Shea, operate off a stall at Spitalfields market. They use a second-hand clothes stall as a front for their gambling business. He is the runner, and she is the banker. The pair of them are worth a small fortune. Staggering, really, considering their backgrounds."

Clarice began to laugh. Her day had suddenly become much better. She'd no idea where to start looking for Joey, but she was thrilled to hear that he had spirit. She liked him, and she'd not even met him yet.

"I will look for him, Mr Hetherington."

He smiled and shook her hand.

"You'll need to be creative if you intend to find him—the little rascal. Keep your wits about you."

Clarice returned the smile.

"I will."

14

THE NIGHT OUT THAT WENT WRONG

Andrew Crouse had not bargained on taking up accommodation in the police station that evening. He found himself sitting on a hard wooden bench with the drunks, pickpockets and crooks. It was a far cry from his soft bed and warm wife.

He'd left home that fine evening to while away the hours in the company of his friends, who had a lot to celebrate. Their underdog football team had won the cup. Their chances of winning were so low that the bookie's odds for success were sky-high. Between them, they had fleeced the bookie that had taken their bet. Someone told Andrew to collect his money from Raffi Fischer's office. Nobody could tell him anything more since Eliza had closed shop in the market a few days ago, and Joey Tophat had disappeared.

Andrew knew his wife Aggie would baulk at the idea of him going on a drinking spree with his winnings. When he popped back home, he told her a little white lie about the size of his stake and said he'd delight in giving her the lion's share. That still left him plenty to celebrate with.

"Aggie, the lads have all won enough money to pay their own way for once. I'll be home early. Promise! Why not get yourself something nice too?"

He pushed the money into her hand and squeezed it tightly.

"Thank you. Promise me you'll be careful?"

He gave her a cheeky wink. He had no intention of being careful. The money had been burning a hole in his pocket ever since he got it. Now, Andrew was hell-bent on having a party with the lads, a party that they would never forget. However, a good night out wasn't in his stars. Had he known how things would pan out, he would undoubtedly have opted to stay with his wife and save his pennies.

The lads agreed to make a night of it at The Bell, a notorious gin palace on Middlesex Street. The landlord often put on a fiddle band and a singer to entertain the throng, and the beer was cheap.

Andrew had an excellent capacity for alcohol. He was by no means inebriated when he bid his friends a cheery goodbye late into the evening.

He left the pub's warmth and the friendly clientele for the city's cold streets, glad that his thick, double-breasted overcoat was buttoned snugly to the throat. He strode along, proud for not surrendering to arm's twisting as his friends tried to convince him to stay for just 'one more.'

Turning the corner, a commotion broke out close by. Looking in the direction of the raised voices, he saw a quarrel across the street that was fast threatening to turn more physical and less vocal.

Andrew admitted to being entertained by the furore, and he stopped to observe the goings-on. His head was clear, and the cold night air burned his nose, but he was inquisitive and stopped to spend a moment observing. It all looked jolly entertaining. He thought of lighting up a cigarette before leaving them to it. While coaxing the matches from his pocket, he was roughly grabbed from behind. Being a cockney chap, his first suspicion was that he'd fallen victim to a pickpocket.

"Oi, what's your game?" he exclaimed with a certain level of indignation.

He wrestled himself free, cursing under his breath, then turned to face his antagonist.

Antagonist though he might be, he was uniformed and therefore entitled to some respect. Surprised, Andrew thought of running off. The officer gave several sharp toots on his whistle to alert the other coppers he needed help. At that moment, Andrew broke free and bolted back around the corner. The officer's head flitted between the fight and the man vanishing round the corner, paralysed with indecision.

Alas, to Andrew's dismay, the policeman had a partner who was also in uniform, answering the call for help. They collided with such force that the other bobby almost lost his footing. The policeman responded angrily, shoving Andrew towards the wall with fierce intent, holding his arm behind his back. The man's instinctive response was to attack, albeit verbally. To his credit, the retaliation was in no way violent, but it was lippy.

> "Constable or not, there is no cause for you to assault me," he said calmly as he attempted to struggle out of the policeman's firm hold on him.

Never one to volunteer to break up an altercation, the first policeman left his colleagues to deal with the problem. Instead, he went to see what the new commotion was. He was met with an angry-looking man demanding the other officer's number.

And that was how Andrew Crouse came to find himself with a policeman on each side, holding him in a vice-like grip. The time for resisting was over. He was marched a few streets away to the police station, where things were about to get worse.

*

It was unusually quiet for a Friday night at the hard-pressed East End constabulary. There were only seventeen men ahead of Andrew. Behind him was a woman. He could see that she wasn't local by her clothes and how she spoke.

"Excuse me, sir," she whispered. "I have never done this before."

"Been arrested? Nor me."

She laughed aloud. Her good humour surprised him, given the dire location. The laugh was contagious, and he couldn't help but smile.

"I am trying to find someone," she said with a hint of misplaced hope.

The girl was quite beautiful and unaffected for someone of her status. There was a warmth about her, a sincerity.

"Come back in the morning, love. It will be quieter then. That's the only advice I have for you."

"I've been standing behind you for three hours. I am not leaving now just to come back and wait for three hours tomorrow."

Andrew nodded his understanding.

"My nephew has gone missing. I need to find him urgently. Actually, he escaped from the workhouse."

"Ha! Good for him. Horrid place."

The man fell silent.

"—There are a lot of missing boys in this city. And, usually, they don't want to be found. I hope you're in luck."

Clarice looked crestfallen.

"Tell me, miss, how did a posh boy find his way into the workhouse?"

"He's not that posh, and he grew up on Dorset Street."

"Mother Mary and all the Saints!"

"My name is Clarice Lawrence."

"Pleased to meet you, luv. I'm Andrew."

Clarice and her new acquaintance waited hours before they got to speak to someone in authority. They were both exhausted, and it was almost dawn.

The arrest took Andrew completely by surprise since he'd merely been an innocent spectator of a not-at-all-illegal fracas on a public street. There had to be witnesses. He'd simply come upon the scene while walking home from a night out. In fact, he was standing across the road from where the incident had taken place. Arguing with the officer afterwards wasn't his finest hour, but harmless enough. He'd soon calmed down.

Finally, Andrew reached the front of the queue. The officer had been on duty for twelve hours and was as exhausted as the rabble before him.

"What's the charge?" the inspector yelled above the noise.

The arresting officer materialised from a grotty looking back room.

"Drunk and disorderly."

In all truth, the copper had forgotten which episode the man had been involved in. It had been a busy night with plenty of drunks to deal with.

"I beg to differ," Andrew argued.

The no-nonsense inspector interrupted him and demanded Andrew's full name, address, and profession. He responded calmly and promptly.

"Get me a statement, Constable Williams, and make it quick. I want to go home." the inspector ordered.

The constable reported that Andrew was drunk and causing an obstruction in the street. He refused to move when asked to politely. Andrew then became 'belligerent' at the request and retaliated by swinging a punch.

Clarice Lawrence paid close attention to every word. She'd been queuing behind Andrew for hours and could bear witness that he'd been sober.

"Is this your wife?"

"No, inspector."

"—I am a witness," Clarice interrupted.

The inspector was abrupt:

"This isn't a courtroom."

"I was on the pavement and watched the incident. This man was startled when a policeman grabbed him from behind. Alone in the dark, I am sure he could be forgiven for thinking he'd encountered a garrotter?"

The inspector stared at Clarice, his face unchanged.

"Could you not have Andrew's sobriety be tested? He displayed no signs of being drunk. After dining out, he'd been on his way home when the constables mistook him for a criminal."

Andrew breathed into his hand and sniffed the exhaled air. He smiled. *'I'll pass a test with ease.'*

To their surprise, the inspector agreed to have a doctor examine Andrew, should he so desire. When Andrew accepted the offer, he went to take a seat.

"Not so fast, Mr Crouse," the investigator
called out. "Pay me the stipulated seven
shilling fine, please, then go to that bench and
wait there. And stay out of my way. You have
caused enough trouble for one night."

Andrew's face dropped. He didn't have seven shillings.
He weighed up the cost of sleeping in gaol or facing the
magistrate in the morning. He would lose a day's wages
and maybe get the sack.

"Will my shillings be refunded once the doctor
has confirmed that I am sober?"

"I have told you that doctors have to be paid.
Depending on the result, you might be
entitled to a partial refund."

"Thank you," Andrew mumbled.

Andrew started digging in his pocket for money he
thought he should still have but somehow didn't. Clarice
interrupted his fidgeting.

"Here. Let me help you. I know that you are
innocent and that I will get my money back."

She put seven shillings into his hand.

"It's a lot of money. I couldn't possibly—"

"It always seems like more if you don't have it.
Here, take it. It's fine."

Andrew wondered where this angel had come from. He was at once ashamed and grateful to have received the help.

"This way, Crouse. Time to join the queue for the doctor."

*

Finally, Clarice had her turn to explain her situation to the inspector. He studied her closely. She was well-spoken, oddly dressed, and gorgeous. He would have been intrigued by her, but he sensed that she was probably trouble.

"Now, what is your complaint, miss?" he sighed.

"My nephew has gone missing, and it's imperative I find him."

"Imperative?"

"Yes. He escaped from Slater Street Workhouse. I need your help to find him."

"Escaped? Well, I never. Alright, what's the lad's name?"

"Joey Cornish."

The inspector's head jerked up.

"Joey Tophat is missing?" he asked, aghast.

"Yes!" Clarice exclaimed. "That's him."

"Everyone knows Little Joey. I will post him as missing right this minute. My men will pay special attention to the case. Joey never causes any trouble. Of course, he's a bit of a rascal, but he's a good lad at heart."

"Thank you, sir."

The inspector smiled at Clarice.

"I hope you find him before we do. Sometimes—"

His voice trailed off. He didn't want to frighten her. The inspector had to concede that as liberal types go, Clarice Lawrence was charming.

"If you wait here a bit, I'll ask some of the lads if they've seen him. He can't go far and not be noticed in that battered top hat of his."

*

A yawning Clarice spotted Andrew over on a bench in the corner, slumped against the wall.

"I have come to say goodbye and good luck."

"You must be tired," said Andrew.

"I am. I haven't slept for more than twenty-four hours. I can't wait to get home."

"How will your husband take to your disappearance?"

"Oh, I'm not married, thank goodness," Clarice chuckled, "much to my mother's chagrin."

"You are different from the women I have met before."

He wanted to add '*of your class*' but didn't want to offend her.

"People say that all the time."

He laughed.

"My wife is going to skin me alive," lamented Andrew.

"I can vouch for you, perhaps?"

"Don't you even dare! Aggie will biff you in the eye. She is a jealous type, and I will be accused of far worse things than I already have."

"Good, then it's our secret."

"I promise to repay you. Please trust me," Andrew said, blushing.

"I know you will. We will worry about that later."

*

Outside, the inky black gloom had turned into grey gloom, which meant that the sun had risen. For a while, Clarice and Andrew stopped talking. They were both lost in their own thoughts. Andrew's main concern was that Aggie would kill him, and Clarice wondered where Joey could be hiding out.

Clarice didn't have the energy to stand up. She leaned back against the red brick wall, closed her eyes, and fell asleep. Her head flopped onto Andrew's shoulder. He didn't want to disturb her, but if anyone told Aggie that he had a woman sleeping on his shoulder, he might as well kill himself there and then and save his wife the trouble.

She slept for thirty minutes until she was jolted awake by a tall man collapsing down beside her. He put his elbows on his knees and dropped his head into his hands. Dozing, he soon toppled against her like a domino. Rousing briefly, he stretched his long legs out in front of him, creating a very unwelcome obstacle in the aisle. Then, he fell into a deep slumber, sparked out in an awkward position.

Once Clarice was sure that he'd passed out, she heaved his body away from her, and he flopped over to the other side. His hat rolled onto the floor, exposing his tousled blond hair. He must have been in his early thirties, no longer a boy. His tanned, rugged face was even more manly because it hadn't seen a razor for a day or two. Other than that, he was reasonably well-dressed, and his hands were not gnarly like a labourer's. She picked up his cap and rested it on his lap, then got a fright when he opened a bleary eye and looked up to thank her.

It took another hour for the doctor to arrive. He spoke to Andrew.

"Come along, mate. The doc's here. Shake a leg,"

The constable turned to the man alongside Clarice and kicked his boot.

"You too. Get up, Jack. Wakey wakey."

The man pushed himself into a sitting position. He seemed to take up all his strength because he promptly closed his eyes again. The constable gave him a good hard shake, and this time the fellow opened his eyes and realised where he was.

"Oh, heavens," he groaned, clutching his head. "What did I do?"

He looked around and then turned to Clarice. He frowned, blinked, and then slowly opened his eyes, allowing the light to torture him a little at a time. Although still blotto, now with his eyes wide open, he was taken aback by the delightful vision.

"Brazen and brave," he slurred. "You are beautiful."

The stranger gave her a dazzling smile. Clarice couldn't place the accent. It was close to Irish, but not quite. His chat with a constable filled in some gaps.

> "The consulate is sending someone, but you won't be allowed to leave until the doctor has examined you. This is the third time you have run amok this month, Wyatt, and your superiors will receive a letter about your behaviour."

Tommo, another officer, gave his unofficial judgement:

> "You don't half do some daft things for such a clever bloke, Jack. You may have diplomatic status, but I reckon that won't be enough to get you off the hook this time."

> "Blood—,"

> "—Mind your language, son.," warned Tommo. "You're in enough hot water as it is."

The curious fellow stood up, donned his hat, and staggered towards the doctor sitting at a corner desk of the charge office. She overheard the two bobbies chatting about him.

> "These Yankees believe they can behave like they do at home. He's a hooligan. If he were a British citizen, he would sit in the nick for two years."

Despite his current condition, Clarice presumed the man led an exotic life. She'd not rubbed shoulders with a diplomat before, not even in the coffee houses near Mayfair's prestigious embassies. She tried to imagine how the fellow might fill his time. Was he a spy? A military man? Who knew?

Soon, Andrew was standing in a different queue, waiting to claim his refund. The doctor took one look at him and passed him off as sober, in good health, and with no physical signs of brawling. The diagnosis suited everyone. Crouse needed to return to his wife, and the two over-zealous arresting officers didn't want a charge of perverting the course of justice.

Clarice was still on the bench and distracted by the American's behaviour. His brief nap on the bench had not improved his condition—the doctor kept snapping at him to pay attention.

His reasons for being hauled in were remarkably similar to Andrew's—drunk and disorderly. But, unlike Crouse, the foreigner was still slurring and appeared to be somewhat off-balance. By usual English standards, the fellow should have been in a cell.

The doctor had no alternative but to declare him severely inebriated.

"This man has been argumentative during the entire examination, sarg."

"I wasn't argumentative," he drawled. "All I did was say you were incompetent and a hopeless station doctor."

The medic was pleased to pass Wyatt on to the next stage of his processing. Clarice strained her ears to follow how things were going.

"This constabulary is harassing me."

"I can assure you that is not the case. Let me ask you again, why did you urinate on a police bicycle?"

"You're making that up."

"Tommo, search him and escort him to the cells, please."

"Right you are, sarg."

Wyatt waited behind bars for the better part of half an hour for someone from the American Consulate to come and fetch him. His condition belied the fact that he might be recognised as a professional of any sort, let alone a diplomat. He assured his rescuer that he was sober and then set about doing nothing to convince the man that he was telling the truth.

His colleague looked on as Jack miraculously walked the entire length of the floor, toe to heel, without faltering. The doctor looked at him in awe. With that accomplished, Wyatt and his escort took leave of the police station, wondering how on earth he'd managed to stay on his feet.

Next to be released was Andrew Crouse. He had used the spare time to check every pocket in his coat. Nothing. Then his fingertips encountered a few loose coins that had slipped through the pocket lining and rolled around the hemline. Thankfully, with this and the rebate, Andrew could clear his debt.

"Thank you for looking after me, Clarice. It could have ended a lot worse than it did without you."

Clarice nodded, grateful for the compliment but not in the mood to chat anymore. All she wanted was to go home and sleep.

"By the way, lass, what is the name of that lad you are looking for again? Perhaps I can keep my ear to the ground?"

"Joey Cornish. He is known as Joey Tophat, apparently. Maybe that's something to do with gambling?"

"I know Joey Tophat!" Andrew exclaimed. "Why didn't you tell me his name to begin with?".

"You never asked."

"Everyone knows Joey—and I know just the person who may have some information."

"I would take you now, but I need to get home to Aggie. Can you meet me at Whitechapel station next Saturday morning? The gaffer lets me finish early if all my work's done for the week. Shall we say ten?"

"Alright. What if the police find him in the meantime?"

"Just leave me a message at the Bell on Middlesex Street. And, long as he turns up, then all's well."

Clarice was grateful for Andrew's help, but next weekend felt a long way away.

15

THE MAGISTRATE'S COURT

Jack Wyatt had to report to the magistrate on Monday. Before then, he was forced to spend more than thirty hours at the embassy, where he was grilled, chastised, and threatened regarding his behaviour. Worse, he wouldn't be allowed to return to his hotel, which had a better bar than the embassy.

When the professor eventually came to his senses, he lay on his bed and looked at the ceiling. He hoped that the press had not heard of his bad behaviour. The last thing he wanted was his shenanigans published. As a learned Harvard scholar, his errant conduct would not go down well in the States either. He ran an ice-cold bath and climbed into it, hoping to feel refreshed and lose his headache. He soon gave up on that. The pain didn't go, and uncontrollable shivering now accompanied it.

It was one-thirty in the afternoon when Jack breakfasted on a cup of the most robust Italian coffee he could find. Then he fled to the library and buried himself in his books. He couldn't escape the ambassador for very long. On the warpath, the man soon sniffed him out.

"Ah, Jack," he said as he pulled out a chair, sat down in front of Wyatt, and stared at him.

Professor Wyatt spoke first.

"I must apologise, sir. The party became quite rowdy."

"All the parties you attend become rowdy. You attend these gatherings in the roughest parts of London. What is the attraction to the hellholes you find yourself in?" the ambassador demanded.

"I like being around ordinary people."

"You do realise you have a good chance of losing your diplomatic status? You'll get no protection from the American flag with this waywardness."

Professor Wyatt gave a slight acknowledgement. The ambassador hit the table with his fist.

"For goodness' sake, man, take this seriously. This isn't a small East Coast town where you are revered for your academic prowess. This is the largest city in the world with the most influential people you will ever meet. Yet you persist in flouting the rules. You're a hooligan, and there is a strong chance that you will be deported this time."

The professor nodded and tried to look as ashamed as he could muster.

"Now pull yourself together by Monday and pray that the magistrate will be lenient. Now, if you excuse me, I need to see my valet."

*

Monday arrived. It was a miserable day. Professor Wyatt was escorted to Bow Street magistrate's court. The building was grey, cold, and dull, just like the weather.

He waited his turn and found himself quite entertained by the stories he heard. When he finally reached the dock, the magistrate had no sympathy for the American.

"Your honour," explained the embassy's solicitor, "this is a diplomatic incident."

The magistrate skimmed the papers he had in front of him.

"Is it? Bawdiness, more like!" roared the magistrate. "Professor Wyatt has been drunk and disorderly five times in the last ten days."

The solicitor sighed inwardly.

"Professor Wyatt will be held in the cells until I have concluded my research with the Foreign Office."

The solicitor began to protest, but it was pointless. The magistrate drowned out the man's voice as he brought down his gavel four times and instructed the bailiff.

"Get him out of my courtroom. Take him to the cells. He will not be bailed."

The accused was then tossed into a cell in the basement of the court building, already inhabited by two inmates. The cell had two bare benches along the longer walls. Every flat surface was etched with earlier captives' initials and their thoughts on confinement. An almost overflowing bucket-style latrine lurked at the far end. *'At least I am with normal people'*, Jack thought.

"Jack Wyatt," he drawled, offering his hand to the fellow to the left.

"Phil Kemp.

"What have you done to end up here, Phil?

"Caused a bit of a rumpus at the pub, me. Got myself arrested. Unreasonable git. I only broke a stool on another fella's noggin. He was asking for it, I swear! And you?"

"Similar," answered Jack Wyatt.

It took some time before the two resigned themselves that they would likely remain confined for quite some time.

"We must reflect that we may have gotten off rather lightly," Phil mused during a lull in the conversation.

"Lightly? Why's that then?" Jack asked with genuine curiosity.

"An old man who worked for my father when I was a small boy told me about his experience with a lock-up in their village. I remember his description well. He said it was just a hole in the ground with a grate on the top. They'd stay there until the hearing."

Professor Jack Wyatt had seen something in a similar pit just outside Alexandria.

"I have heard them called roundhouses, the cage, the lobby, watch house, blind house, and the clink. Purpose-built, small, either square, rectangular, or octagonal. I was kept in one for five days straight when I worked in Egypt. Little swines those Egyptians at times. No sense of humour. The place was sweltering. Flies buzzing everywhere. It had no windows, only a ventilation grille over the pit."

"Sounds awful."

"And then some," said Jack, pulling a face. "I had to spend five nights in that hole. It was as hot as hell. There wasn't a scrap of fresh air."

"How did you end up in there?" Phil asked, fascinated.

"It turns out flirting with the Sultan's daughter gets you locked up for a week. Still, I count myself lucky, though. Other offenders who were convicted around that time were facing a death sentence or having their hands cut off."

"Thanks for telling me that story."

"Really?"

"Yes. It's making this place look like the Ritz."

Jack Wyatt laughed at Phil's comment, pleased his sense of humour was returning.

This was what people couldn't understand about the American. He would rather discuss this with an ordinary bloke than with an academic debate. He had been raised in a humble family in West Virginia. If it had not been for a schoolteacher who took a liking to him and saw his potential, he would still be living under the Blue Ridge Mountains. Although he had a wild streak, he appreciated his blessings. Unlike other professionals with a string of qualifications, his most outstanding achievement was buying his parents a small farm near Harvard. It had cost him an arm and a leg, as well as a loan from the bank, but it was all worth it when he saw the beaming smiles of his parents.

"I found out that the roundhouse in which they kept the prisoners is now used by the parish council as a mortuary," Phil said, returning to his story from the old man.

"So, we might see our end there someday after all." Jack Wyatt joked. "Was the old man found not guilty by the magistrate?"

"He never faced the magistrate," Phil explained with a chuckle. "That is the best part of the story. By fluke, someone found out the back door key of the pub also fitted the padlock on the bars at the lock-up. The landlady would liberate the drunks after the constable went home. It was a great little system. The prisoners got their freedom, and the landlady sold a lot of beer to the grateful throng that frequented there."

*

The magistrate was determined to make an example of Jack Wyatt. He sent a message to the Foreign Office saying he would contact them to discuss the matter within the next few days. He didn't want a diplomatic circus in his court. Wyatt needed to learn some manners.

The conversation had run dry by the early morning hours, and the men felt deflated. It was around nine o'clock that Phil's name was called. Someone had come forward and said another man had caused the affray, and the case against Phil was quickly dismissed.

The other man in the cell was called a little later, leaving Wyatt alone to reflect on his situation. Mid-week the drunk and disorderly cases often plummeted.

It was approaching four in the afternoon, and Wyatt was sure he would be waiting another day. It was then he was summoned to appear. The charges were read out, and the defence solicitor called for the ambassador's valet. The valet and all of his team acted as one, testifying they were sure Wyatt didn't urinate on the bicycle, and it was a case of mistaken identity. The embassy's medical officer said the professor was stone-cold sober when he returned after the supposed incident. The judge knew it was a cover-up but was powerless, given they were all providing *'sworn testimonies.'* The arresting officer's evidence simply didn't match all the other depositions, tying the magistrate's hands.

> "The British legal system is ashamed that it
> cannot penalise you for your poor behaviour.
> I am gravely disappointed that there isn't
> enough evidence to imprison you for a
> minimum of three months. Let this be a
> warning to you, Professor Wyatt. If you are

convicted of being drunk and disorderly
again, your diplomatic status shall be revoked,
and you will be placed in the care of Her
Majesty's prison service. Take him down."

The usher grabbed Jack roughly by the arm and dragged him out of the courtroom. He was given his belongings and shoved out onto the street. Relieved to escape and avoid a stretch in Wormwood Scrubs, Jack noticed it was a little sunnier than the day before, and he hoped it was a good sign. Being free was good, and so too was avoiding a reprimand from the ambassador or his superiors at Harvard.

He was due to give a lecture at the British Museum in the coming days, and he needed to prepare his notes. The American Metropolitan Museum of Art had shipped an Assyrian artefact to London as an act of goodwill, and he'd been sent with it. His knowledge of ancient history was immense, plus he'd played a significant role in deciphering the ancient writing on it. Now, all he had to do was give the talk and keep his nose out of trouble.

Keeping up appearances, the ambassador welcomed him back into the embassy as if they were long-lost friends. Interfering with witnesses and lying on oath were not discussed.

"Thank you for understanding, sir," said Wyatt.

"Just please stay out of trouble, Jack. Please? Now, about this lecture of yours—"

16

THE PATROL

The wintery weather was setting in. Yesterday's sunshine was a faded memory. A crisp layer of frost lay on the ground, peppered with jet black cinders. The streetlamps were dull, their glow barely visible in the foul weather. There was only one lonely figure in Great Russell Street, a man wearing a long coat, hat, and a scarf. The shadowy figure was bent forward as he fought through the bitter wind funnelled by the tall London streets.

Eventually, he reached his destination. His hands were so cold that he struggled to grip the key in his stiff fingers. He avoided the main entrance and paced to an annexe which hid a private entrance. The man wriggled the key in the lock, opened the heavy door, and stepped inside. He sighed with relief. He was home.

Malcolm Featherstone had been the custodian of the British Museum for twenty years. He began his career as a young man, eager and determined to please his masters. His first appointment was behind the scenes as a cleaner in the archives. The documents and priceless artefacts in the museum's care had to be maintained in a cool, dry, and insect-free environment. Here, he learned the history of almost every exhibit in the building. It was a delight and a privilege to see the items rather than stare at them through a display case's cold, thick glass.

His superiors were happy with his performance as a cleaner and deemed him fit for promotion. His knowledge of the displays meant an appointment as a concierge. He hated standing at the majestic front doors, tipping his hat to all and sundry. Try as he might to be demoted back to a cleaner, he failed. After a long year, he was promoted to chief steward because of his familiarity with the premises and strong work ethic. His enthusiasm for the exhibits was infectious, and the other room stewards loved to work with him. He was delighted to be back inside, admiring the treasures on display once more. During the occasional lulls in the day, he took advantage of these quiet moments to study an exhibit. If a relic perplexed him, he would sneak off to the luxurious reading room during his lunch hour and investigate the matter further. Malcolm's rise in status and opportunity was quite a feat for an ordinary man who had been educated in a humble school.

The greatest day in Featherstone's career was when he was appointed museum custodian, responsible for maintaining every inch of the building and managing the labourers who did the work. He was proud and dedicated to his position, working day and night to ensure that the stately building was kept pristine. Although he was a fair man, woe betide anyone who didn't respect the building or its exhibits. Any laxness or complacency amongst his staff was swiftly dealt with.

Thanks in part to his work, the British Museum was recognised as one of the world's most magnificent museums, showcasing artefacts gathered from all the great empires of history. It was also the world's first public museum. Oh, how he delighted in bringing the treasures within to the masses.

During his tenure, the building had undergone many changes, including the library's relocation and the addition of new wings providing new homes for the expanding collection.

He had changed too. Over the years, Featherstone became more scholarly—and more possessive of his ward. All the little slip-ups in daily operations made him worried. That worry turned into a secret distrust of his staff. In his mind, things got missed unless he oversaw all the little details. It started to anger him. He lost trust in the academic staff members, who were more interested in studying and less interested in the management of the place. So fanatical was he that he'd nurtured the habit of being the first person to arrive at the museum in the morning and the last person to leave at night.

Lately, his increasingly obsessive dedication didn't endear him to anyone, making them even less likely to follow his long list of demands. It marked the start of a downward spiral in relations. People began to loathe the tall, gaunt figure that loomed in the shadows and appeared out of nowhere. As he became more confrontational, the staff became more critical.

Although staff preferred to avoid Featherstone, the donors and patrons extolled him. The wealthy bestowed and bequeathed their collections to the museum, secure in the knowledge that the fastidious custodian was overseeing them.

Featherstone also cut a lonely figure in his home life. His wife had died some years ago, and his children had grown up and flown the nest. They seldom saw their father, nor did they want to. He'd always been too preoccupied with his job to show them any real kindness. Secretly, he didn't see his life as lonely. He was pleased no one clung to him for their existence. It freed him up to give all his time and attention to the most remarkable institution in the world, a place that Malcolm Featherstone no longer thought of as the 'British' Museum—but his.

*

For some time now, the custodian had developed an odd intuition that he wasn't alone. As he did his last round of inspections every night, he had a strange sensation that there was someone else there. He drafted strongly worded letters to the various departments, demanding to know if anyone had recently spent time in the museum at night. All advised him no one had.

Featherstone refused to accept defeat. His first thought was that an intruder was lurking, and a robbery was being planned. His second idea was that an office romance had developed between two employees and that they were using the premises to meet after hours. The idea of anyone desecrating his sacred domain to satisfy their secret pleasures disgusted him.

It was time to devise a strategy to identify and capture the culprit.

IIe set about creating a secret plan to increase his vigilance. Without telling anyone else, he began to leave the museum after midnight instead of his usual hour of ten o'clock. The custodian would take his torch and walk from room to room every night. He changed his route through the building each time to avoid being predictable and only left the building when he was as sure as he could be that everything was in order.

On one of these evenings, he made his discovery and finally gained proof that the trespassers were not a couple in the throes of a romantic tryst but something far more sinister.

Featherstone went to inspect the last room for the night. He opened a heavy, carved door and entered the cavernous dining room. Holding up his lamp, he slowly took a tour of the room. He bent over and looked under each table in case someone was hiding under it. He was satisfied that he'd been thorough in his search. But as he looked up, he got the fright of his life. On the wall opposite him was a fleeting but gigantic shadow of a man. There was no silhouette of the face. All he could recognise was some sort of brimmed hat. He looked again, but the vision was gone. It mattered not. He might have only seen the apparition momentarily, but at last, he was sure his intuition was correct. A logical, educated man, not prone to superstition, he knew that he'd seen the shadow of a man and not an apparition— and since it was human, he would trap the intruder forthwith and hand him over to the police.

*

Featherstone made his way to the guard's room, where he promptly summoned all the watchmen.

"Gentlemen, we have an intruder."

At first, the men secretly ridiculed him, pulling faces at each other and stifling their laughter.

"I saw a man's shadow in the dining room. He was wearing a top hat. I don't know what he is planning, but we must capture him forthwith."

The mood changed. One of the younger men looked terrified.

"But we check the building thoroughly, Mr
Featherstone. It can't be a man. What if it's a
mummy that's come back to life? The ghost of
a Pharaoh coming back to haunt us!"

The watchmen were not well-educated men in an era
when much attention was given to spiritualism and
mediums. Terrifyingly destructive ideas had already
seeped into their minds. The men's eyes widened and
darted around them, looking for the evil presence.

"Now listen to me. Clear your minds of any
silly notions. There are no ghosts or
phantoms in the building. The dead animals
and mummified figures are just that—dead."

His reassurance came too late. Unease had turned to
dread, soon to escalate to terror. This outright fear of
the dead made them more incompetent than usual.

"We must catch this man."

He advised them of the route they should take, and the
men dispersed. They appeared to be methodical when
Featherstone watched them, but as soon as he was out
of sight, they would huddle in small groups. There was
safety in numbers.

Whitey Smith had only been employed as a watchman
for three months. His energetic approach had
impressed Mr Featherstone at first. Whitey was young
and overconfident and always boasted about his
fearlessness in the boxing ring. According to Whitey, he

never got thumped. After the fight, his opponents always went home with black eyes or broken noses. The other blokes at work were sceptical of his success. On this evening, their scepticism proved correct. They could all testify that Whitey was a coward and had run from the building, even paler than his name suggested.

Whitey opened a gilded door and entered a magnificently decorated space the size of a ballroom. He didn't feel overly anxious because the room had no specimens of the dead. Instead, it held stunning antiques, tapestries and the like. Whitey dawdled down the centre of the room, trying to waste sufficient time and avoid being dispatched into the more eerie bowels of the building. He stopped. Some fabric overlaying the items looked crumpled. Despite the do not touch signs, some members of the public just couldn't help themselves. It drove Featherstone to distraction. Whitey assumed that one of the maids had been slack. *'Ha! I'll get Featherstone to sack her and suggest my Elsie fills her shoes. Gawd knows we need the money.'*

Whitey stepped over the velvet rope that separated him from the display, intent on disturbing the area a little more to drive his point home. He put his hand down and touched the offending display, then pulled his hand away as if he'd been burnt. Something was in the middle of the bedclothes. Whitey bent over to take a closer look. A curious pale object lay on the top. Horrified, he saw a hand severed from its arm at the wrist in front of him.

Featherstone heard Whitey's shriek echo down the corridors of the museum. Within moments, all the watchmen were sprinting towards the sound of the cries, the heels of their heavy boots giving the perfectly polished parquet floors a hammering. Featherstone was breaking as he imagined the damage they were doing to his pristine surface. Bursting into the room, they saw Whitey over at the far wall, shaking like a leaf.

"What is this all about, Smith?" Featherstone demanded

"Sir, there is a hand in the cloth!" Whitey exclaimed, pointing to it.

Hysterical, Whitey couldn't keep his voice down. The terror raised his tone a couple of octaves.

"There is a victim. And that means a murderous spirit in this room," Whitey panted. "We must find somebody to exorcise it."

The phrase, 'murderous spirit' made the hair rise on the back of their necks. No one moved.

Whitey was satisfied that he'd done his duty by alerting Featherstone to the severed hand. Without excusing himself, he took flight. He escaped into the corridor and ran as if the devil was chasing him, and he didn't stop until he was out of the building. The hysteria was contagious. His colleagues followed in Whitey's footsteps and didn't look back.

Mr Featherstone found himself standing alone in the middle of the room. He stepped towards the bed and inspected the severed hand. The old custodian didn't have a good sense of humour, but when he realised he was looking at an ivory-coloured glove, he began to laugh. Standing beside the majestic Jacobean bed, Malcolm couldn't stop laughing.

In time, his mind turned to how the glove got there and why the bedclothes were in such disarray. Convinced the garment wasn't present, nor the display so dishevelled when he conducted his solo patrol earlier, the disturbance was more proof of the prowler. He grinned.

He didn't care what lengths he would have to go to, but he would solve the mystery—and when he did, there would be serious repercussions. No punishment would be too generous for the felon who dared to disturb the sanctity of his empire.

17

THE CURIOUS DELIVERY

Professor Abercrombie looked at his custodian and frowned. The man was ruining his morning by complaining about someone prowling the museum after hours. The professor had just received a crate which held a magnificent Babylonian tablet. It stood in the store waiting to be unpacked.

"Utter piffle, Malcolm, and I simply don't have time forrit. The glove was probably dropped by a visitor or a cleaner."

Featherstone bit his bottom lip. His veins pulsed in his temples. The devoted custodian looked at the younger man before him. He'd never liked the cocky little twirp. Why Abercrombie had been appointed was a mystery. There were plenty of highly qualified professors in England who would have been better suited to the job. The professor's Geordie accent grated on his ear. His loud, pompous demeanour was loathsome. All in all, Featherstone found the fellow repugnant.

"With respect, that's where you are wrong, professor. The glove belonged to Lord Nelson.

A priceless item. How it got out of the display case is a mystery."

"I agree. That is puzzlin'."

"Furthermore, we established that fruit and biscuits were missing from the kitchen pantry. The cook says the larder door is often ajar when he arrives in the morning. He is adamant he closes it nightly."

"The missing food is the work o' rats," Abercrombie said dismissively.

"Rats cannot open doors, drop gloves, crumple bed clothes or wear a hat—" Mr Featherstone countered angrily. "—But an intruder can."

"Fiddlesticks. I suggest you begin yer investigation with the obvious. Clearly, you have a thief on your staff."

Undeterred by the slur, Featherstone continued.

"I need your assistance to trap the culprit. If we appoint a watchman for every room, we will flush out the intruder within days. It will be a temporary arrangement."

"You are asking me to fritter away my budget trying to catch a non-existent intruder? May I ask—How old are you, sir? Perhaps you are going senile?"

Malcolm's fury began to boil over. Here was a man attempting to portray him as unprofessional and stupid, and he knew he was neither.

"Go about your job more professionally," the young man droned. "Have you considered early retirement? Else, I must enlighten the board o' me concerns."

Featherstone knew that arguing would make no difference. Abercrombie wouldn't listen to him. He'd never been so seriously threatened in the workplace before, and it caught him off guard. After dedicating most of his life to the institution, he would be shattered if he were dismissed by a Geordie upstart.

"Away wi' ya now. Run along, Mr Featherstone. I am sure you have more important things to do."

The custodian looked as angry as a bull about to charge.

"Please ensure that all the exhibits are pristine and not in the untoward state you found them last night. It goes without saying, the board will take a dim view of anyone lettin' our precious collection be neglected. I have a duty of care—"

Although the professor was mid-sentence, Featherstone turned and left, his nose out of joint. Striding down the corridor, he vowed never to surrender to his nemesis. *'That pompous fool needs to fall down the stairs and break both his legs—or his neck.'*

*

Even though his request for extra watchmen had been denied, the custodian's mind was still compelled to work out what was going on. The answer was simple. He would move into the museum. Nobody would need to know about it. If the strange man with a top hat could live inside the stately building without being noticed, so could he.

Featherstone hid several days' worth of food in his desk. Then he found a tiny storeroom, unused for years, and shoved a battered old sofa to one side, perfect for sleeping on. After their recent fright, many of the guards had resigned, and he was sure the remaining watchmen wouldn't find him. They were too terrified to wander to the far corners of the place now.

Recruitment began apace, and hundreds of job applications arrived each day. Soon, the area was infested with men arriving for interviews, with Featherstone insisting that he interview each applicant. His artefacts were irreplaceable, and he gladly took up the responsibility of ensuring that the new staff were trustworthy—and had the nerve to flush out the interloper.

18

A NIGHT ON THE TOWN

Forever precocious, Joey's growing confidence led him to wander around the place more often. Soon he'd seen all the delights in all the rooms. He was living well in the museum. What more could a lad on the run wish for?

Going about his adventures, he finally found a flight of stairs which led him down to a door with a sign on it. The sign read, "Archives—Staff only—Keep Out." He tried the handle, but it was locked. As he turned to leave, he saw the glow of a lamp at the top of the staircase. At first, he thought it was a watchman, then he heard voices. Two men were deep in conversation. One of the men had a Geordie accent, and the other man was a foreigner.

Panicking, Joey backtracked and squeezed in behind a giant wooden crate.

"I am rather excited to see this Assyrian tablet, professor." said the foreigner.

"Yes. It is rather wonderful. We are lucky to have it. And Heinrich, call me Paul. I think we can be less formal now."

"Entschuldigung. We Germans are very formal. You are right—business partners must be friends."

The two men passed the crate and made their way to the archive door. Joey heard the key rattling in the keyhole, and the colossal lock sprung open. The lad's heart beat faster. The door creaked open, and the two men crept inside. Suddenly, Joey heard a voice in the distance, a guard on patrol.

"Hello? Who's down there?"

Abercrombie responded.

"It's just me and Professor Raubach. All is well. We are working late. Got a talk to give tomorrow."

"Very well, sir. Don't work too late now. Night."

The footsteps faded, and Joey began to relax. He heard the archive door bang shut, and he planned to move on until he heard the footsteps of the two men walking towards the great crate.

"This tablet is a gift. Unfortunately, it belongs to the Americans. We have it on loan from them. They have sent a Harvard man with it as if we don't know what we are doing. He is quite the academic over there. Jack Wyatt?"

"Ja, I have heard of him."

"A bit of a loose cannon by all accounts, which is rather fortuitous since I have three buyers for this item already," bragged Abercrombie. "We can make our price."

"Four. A German prince is desperate to buy it too."

"We'll never have to work again," Abercrombie joshed. "Just think—we'll be able to drink good wine and chase fine French women on sunny rivieras for the rest of our lives."

"Why not retire to the Polynesian Islands? I believe that native women are far less uninhibited. We will have no need to dig through sand to earn a living."

Abercrombie looked at Raubach in disappointment.

"Now, now, Heinrich. You mustn't say things like that. You must learn to love digging in the sand. Remember, every time we dig, we get rich. There is quite a demand for antiquities on the black market."

This time it was Heinrich's turn to laugh.

"This prince. How much is he prepared to spend with us?"

"I've hinted at one million marks."

"It looks like we have our buyer then," said the smug Geordie, gaining even greater respect for his partner in crime.

"But, how will we get it out of here, Paul? The guards. They patrol everywhere?"

"Simple. It leaves precisely as it arrived. But instead of going to America, it's going to get lost at the East India Dockyard. It will start out like this but will end up disguised as a crate of spices then vanish—only to appear at the door of a great castle in Germany."

"You have thought of everything."

"We are always transferring artefacts between museums. The Americans at the Metropolitan museum are such a decent bunch they would never expect a Brit to steal a national treasure. It is wonderful to work with such naive people. We simply send it to the wrong place—by, err, mistake. There's not much they can do if we have papers proving we sent it to the correct destination. A few quid to one of those drunken dockers to change a few details, stick a label on, and we're good to go."

Both men lingered around the displays in the far corner, but Joey wasn't inclined to wait any longer after hearing their bold scheme. If they knew someone had overheard, they would be keen to silence the eavesdropper. He squeezed out from behind the crate and made a bid to flee, holding onto his jiggling top hat as he went.

"Hey, you!" yelled Paul. "Stop!"

Joey turned around to look at them. Then, he panicked and shot along the corridor that led back to the larder. He looked behind, and the coast seemed clear. There were so many doors off the long, winding corridor that he could have chosen he must have shaken off his pursuers. He grabbed two celebratory apples from the kitchen. He slipped into the dining room and received his second shock of the night. Another person came out of the shadows. The boy stood dead still. The man hadn't noticed him. Yet.

The fellow dropped down on all fours and swept his arms under the tables, looking for someone or something. Joey's imagination ran away with him, convinced that one of the professors had found him after all.

Panicking again, Joey ran. He ran right across the room and somehow managed to escape. The figure leapt to its feet and lifted a torch. The beam swept the room. Joey saw the light illuminate the wall next to him. He didn't stop.

"Everyone, in here now!" yelled the observer.

By the time Featherstone's beam reached the door, he was dismayed to see the intruder was gone. Yet, despite being given the slip, the old custodian was relieved. Yes, he'd been ridiculed by Professor Abercrombie, but he'd seen the shadow again by the dining area. Someone else might have seen him in the corridor. Whoever the intruder was had to eat, and Mr Featherstone would either starve him or catch him.

Joey scarpered back to the canopy bed and silently slithered into his secret sanctuary. Thankfully, he'd not dropped any of the food he'd pilfered from the kitchen as he fled. He pulled the panel back up, sat in the darkness, and considered his options. There were few. He couldn't live inside the museum forever with that shadowy figure on the prowl. Outside, the workhouse staff wanted to hunt him down too. It would just be a matter of time before someone caught him. The only question was—who? There was also the added complexity of the overheard conversation. If the greedy Geordie suspected the intruder had overheard the discussion near the archives, he was as good as dead anyway.

*

Paul Abercrombie lay back in a battered old chair, its upholstery full of holes. Nobody had seen a need to fix it as the brothel didn't cater to clientele who were interested in aesthetics. The young professor had promised his German associate an entertaining night on the town, and he was determined not to disappoint.

Professor Raubach was in love with London, principally the slums. He'd found that the more sophisticated brothels were somewhat 'particular' about how a customer treated one of their workers, but in the city's darker corners, the cheaper establishments and lone women, in particular, would do anything for money.

He didn't have the same freedom in Heidelberg. The whole town knew him, the women were unimaginative, and he had a stoic Bavarian wife, Helga. Her father had been an officer who had given them a strict Lutheran upbringing. Heinrich didn't know why he'd married the cold woman. He couldn't lay his strange appetites at her door—a door she'd firmly shut except to conceive four well-disciplined children.

The most noticeable difference between the upmarket and lower-class establishments was their choice of dress. Contrary to traditional female dress, prostitutes always wore gowns made from shiny bright material that shimmered in the light and accentuated their figures. Heinrich wondered why high-society women had to be so dowdy. In addition, the working girls also abandoned the custom of wearing bonnets and shawls in public. Their hair hung loose, and their shoulders were bare, waiting to be caressed. These delicious creatures could enter places like pubs, taverns, and bars without the social stigma that a 'lady' would carry.

Although the sophisticated London brothels had their immaculate facilities catered to the elite, Heinrich found them boring and restrictive.

The brothels in Whitechapel were far more to his liking because the lowest class of young women worked in them. They were forced to sleep with whichever man the madame assigned to them and mostly had unpleasant living conditions. The prostitutes in a brothel community protected each other but were more flexible than their upmarket sisters. To Heinrich's delight, despite the impoverished conditions, most had a dodgy doctor on-site, which meant he wouldn't return home in a poor state of health. He wished that other countries were this progressive. He'd picked up a nasty little bug in Cairo.

"Does it meet your requirements?" asked Abercrombie.

"More than you can imagine."

"Of course, you have a wide choice of services. Can I introduce you to some of these?"

Raubach shook his head.

"I believe I can negotiate my way around a whorehouse, my good man!"

There were a variety of brothels dedicated to different styles of pleasure, some more palatable than others for two hot-blooded men. Places that encouraged a chap to wear women's clothes were somewhat off-putting. Establishments that dished out whippings were not to Raubach's taste as he didn't enjoy pain.

This particular brothel specialised in young girls and virgins, which came with its own merits. Since the two men genuinely feared venereal disease, they preferred maidens. It guaranteed they wouldn't risk losing their manhood to disease. Only wealthy men could afford to deflower a girl. The two professors had plenty of money, and they could well afford the luxury.

Some of the most frequent customers at brothels were young men in the military. Although they were young, they were regular patrons and often developed some affection for the ladies they patronised.

'Madame du Puy' didn't have a drop of French blood running through her veins. Her real name was Hetty Crick, and her pub on the bottom floor fed the brothel upstairs.

Seven very young girls worked there, each portraying the roles of inexperienced virgins nightly. She kept track of who came to visit and which girl they bought. These young women were well paid because the job also included over-the-top acting and a hefty dose of discretion. With a combination of slivers of chicken liver and a great deal of sobbing and begging for the end to come, the young women did a roaring trade.

Professor Raubach looked at the young girl cowering on the bed before him. Her eyes were wide with fright, and she huddled her nude figure behind the bedstead for protection. Her hands were clasped around the black iron, the knuckles white. Heinrich loved the look of fear, and poor Amy looked terrified.

"Heinrich," said Madame du Puy, "meet Amy. Amy Brown. She's a little orphan off the streets of Manchester. Nobody will look for the child since nobody cares. I can assure you there will be no repercussions whatsoever."

"Wunderbar," muttered the German, his gaze never leaving the girl's direction.

The story was a complete lie, of course. Amy Brown, alias Violet Douglas, was a nineteen-year-old who had lived in the East End her entire life. She was petite and red-headed. Her chest, at its current stage of development, was still flat. Nude, she looked almost pre-pubescent, yet, dressed, Raubach would never have recognised her on the streets of Whitechapel.

While Raubach was resting between bouts of abusing Violet, he would enjoy a cognac with Abercrombie. Instead of the discussion being focused on their current carnal activities with the girls, they discussed their business

"We can have as many young maidens as we like after selling our treasure," whispered Raubach.

"Wyatt must not get a whiff of our plan to steal his precious Abyssinian stone," Paul warned. "Just because the Americans are naive, it doesn't stop them giving us very long gaol sentences if they catch someone stealing their property."

"It isn't stealing—more, hmm—losing," mused Raubach. "I'm happy to lose a crate for a million pounds. Aren't you?"

Paul noted a pair of feet peeping out below the curtain that cordoned off access to the second floor.

"We shouldn't be talking about this," he said, nodding towards the potential eavesdropper.

The curtain swung open, and a naked Violet appeared, seemingly unaware of their chat.

"I am sorry to interrupt, Professor Heinrich. Madame du Puy asks if you are ready to lie with me again?"

"Most definitely. Go. Make yourself ready."

He leaned over to Abercrombie.

"Relax, she is just a child. She has no inkling of what we were discussing."

But, oh, how wrong he was. Violet Douglas was shrewd for someone not yet twenty. Early in her career, she'd learned that information was far more valuable than prostitution. If she heard any gossip that could earn her a few pounds, she would sell it to Emilio Luca, the Italian barber. What happened after that wasn't her business. Luca was good to her, and she, in turn, was a loyal informer. For now.

19

THE INFORMER

The good weather had given way to a foul wind; soot and dust blew in the air, and midday could have been late evening. Emilio saw Violet loitering outside the barbershop, modestly dressed. To an onlooker, there was no indication of what she did for a living.

The Latino man felt sorry for the girl, but not pity. It wasn't a choice but an unfortunate set of circumstances that forced her hand. He respected her for turning an otherwise soul-destroying job into a lucrative trade in intelligence. He sensed in his bones that as soon as Violet had enough money saved up to leave Madame du Puy, she would be off for good.

Emilio took a drag on his dwindling cigarette and opened the shop door. He stepped outside, acknowledged Violet, and then nodded to the right, indicating they should make their way down the alley for more privacy.

"Ciao, Viol—"

The girl had no time for small talk and got to the point.

"Something interesting happened with a German customer last night."

"A kraut, you mean."

"Not now, Emilio. You know I haven't got long," she sighed.

"I wish you'd leave that place. I look after you, don't I?"

"Only when I bring you news. If I leave, then what?"

Emilio flicked his fading cigarette to the floor and stamped on it. His Latin blood made him emotional and murderous. She never believed him when he said he found Crick and her sordid operation loathsome.

"I keep telling you it won't be forever. I might sell this place one day and whisk you away to Sicily. How about that?"

Violet smiled wryly. Emilio was always sweet to her, but it was only words. She was used to his good intentions spawning false promises.

"You are a sweetheart, but that's nonsense."

"Alright. Have it your way. So, tell me then. What did you hear?" Emilio asked as he lit up another smoke.

"Two professors, one was a German visitor, and the other works at the London Museum—"

"—And that's it?" the Italian said, looking bored. "At a push, these academicos could be blackmailed—or, no, hang on, maybe they'll just deny everything?"

Everyone knew how easy it was for a wealthy man to seek justice against a female blackmailer in court. The defence was a simple one. Why wouldn't a destitute and immoral fallen woman make the whole thing up to augment her meagre earnings?

"I'm sorry, but there will be no money in it."

"Hush! You don't understand. It's not visiting Hetty that is interesting. It's the private discussion I overheard while they were there."

"And?"

"They are planning to steal something valuable from the museum."

"A painting—?"

"—No."

Violet glared at Emilio. His constant interruptions were wearing thin.

"A stone relic of some sort. It's from an old country. Like Egypt but not Egypt. It has some writing on it. They want to sell it to somebody in Germany."

"Are you sure? You are not making a mistake?"

"I promise. You know I don't make mistakes when it comes to something serious."

Emilio stroked his chin as they walked back to the barbershop without saying a word. He fumbled for his wallet and took out some money. This will do for now.

"I'll tell the boss. If we make something out of it, you'll get your share."

Violet smiled, and for the first time that afternoon, Emilio smiled back at her.

"Stop working for that witch and come away with me. You'll love Sicily."

"Stop teasing. It's incredibly annoying."

Emilio looked at her with piercing eyes then said:

"I'm not."

"And what will I do there, prithee? Sell lemons in the marketplace? Tend to your family's goats all day?"

"Do you want to live the rest of your life pretending you are a virgin to grubby men? Do you want chicken liver running down your legs every night? You're not getting any younger, you know. You will work past this place one day, and I will be gone, back to my homeland."

Violet tried to argue that it was her life and her choice, but it was useless. Emilio's Italian blood was raging. He threw his hands in the air and stalked off, too angry to say goodbye. Emilio always joked with her, but today, for some reason, he was deadly earnest.

20

ELIZA O'SHEA

Andrew Crouse was as good as his word. He was standing outside Whitechapel station at ten o'clock sharp on the Saturday. It amused him that he'd made such good friends while at the police station, and he was grateful for his kind companion covering his fee.

Clarice climbed off the train and saw Andrew waving his hat high in the air, and she rushed towards him. He greeted her with a big smile.

"Hello, Miss Lawrence."

"We are meeting under far better circumstances than last time." she joked. "Thank you for offering to help. I have had no luck searching for Joey, and the police drew a blank."

"No matter lass, we will do our best. What are friends for?"

Andrew took the lead, and Clarice followed. They walked through the warren of dark, narrow streets until they reached a slender building. There was a plate on the pillar next to the door. Raffi Fischer, Private Banker, 2nd Floor. Crouse shook his head at the sign.

"Private banker. Utter tosh. He's a moneylender."

"Oh!"

Rebecca Fischer didn't often warm to people, but she liked Clarice Lawrence from the moment they were introduced.

"My husband likes your cousin very much. He is an excellent businessman and has a lot of integrity."

"But he is only a child," said Clarice, astonished.

"Since he survived a few years on Dorset Street, he must have the wisdom of a forty-year-old."

Andrew nodded in agreement.

"Do you know anything else about him?" Clarice asked.

"He was in business with a woman named Eliza O'Shea. He made Raffi promise that he would take care of Eliza until he got back. Eliza is beside herself with worry. He has been gone for several days now—"

Raffi Fischer emerged from his office.

"Ah, you must be Miss Lawrence!"

He looked tired, and he was. He didn't really want to discuss Joey. He'd happily taken care of Eliza. He had read in the paper that the lad had escaped from the workhouse, but he was convinced that the boy was safe and would soon pop up when the coast was clear.

Clarice offered her hand.

"Mr Fischer!"

"None of that. I am Raffi. Has Rebecca offered you a cup of tea yet? We can sit and talk."

No sooner had the tea been poured into the delicate porcelain cups than there was a knock at the door, and it was opened.

"I tried to—" said Rebecca, peering over the man's shoulder

"It is almost Rosh Hashana, Raffi."

Raffi anticipated the lecture and made plans to flee.

"Shalom, rabbi."

The rabbi pulled a face.

"Shalom Raffi, I see you are busy taking people's money again."

"Not at all. You have caught me in the middle of a mitzvah, rabbi. I must be off."

The rabbi grunted with disdain.

"A mitzvah isn't a mitzvah if you go around telling everyone."

"Yes, rabbi. Now, Andrew, Clarice, shall we?"

Raffi, desperate to avoid having another strip torn off by the rabbi, herded the pair out of his office.

"I thought you wanted tea," said Rebecca, annoyed at the sight of the abandoned refreshments.

"Sorry, my darling, we have no time for tea. This matter is life or death. Come with me, Miss Lawrence. We cannot waste time. Goodbye, rabbi. We shall speak next week, no doubt."

Raffi Fischer hustled Clarice and Andrew down the stairs, terrified of another hour of grilling from the rabbi.

He only stopped to talk to his guests when they were well away from his office and to catch his breath.

*

"Where are we going?" Clarice asked.

"To meet Eliza O'Shea." wheezed Raffi. "She is Joey's business partner, mentor, and friend. It is an unusual relationship, but this is how the poor survive. If he's got a message to anyone, it'll be her."

"Excellent!"

"Look for a second-hand clothes stall. There will be men and women hanging round it."

Few areas in the city could be compared with the vibrance of the Spitalfields Market, and Clarice took in everything around her. The heart of it, the Horner Building, looked magnificent, a vast mock-Tudor masterpiece. The place was teeming with buyers and street sellers. The hawkers, costermongers, and stallholders had taken up every available space in the surrounding streets, including the pavement and the road. Delivery boys with wobbly sack barrows and irate cart drivers fought through the throng to access the main entrance, a lofty archway towering above them. It was bedlam.

Clarice's preliminary research into Joey had confirmed that the area was desperately poor. She decided it would be best to plump for understated attire and dressed in a warm grey skirt and blouse covered with a navy coat. Her knitted scarf made of brightly coloured odds and ends of yarn looked cheery. Her hat was a scruffy velvet one. She'd sat on it one time too many, and its formal life was over. The look was perfect. She didn't look impoverished, but she didn't look rich either. She could melt into the crowd without worrying about pickpockets and other ne'er-do-wells. The warmth in the casual exchanges of the poor was a delight. Everyone knew each other, and although every day meant a slog just to survive, the mood was jovial.

On the whole, the shoppers were an army of housewives flooding the area, tightly wrapped against the chill with thick, fringed black shawls around their shoulders. Little boys tried to lure customers with the wares they had to sell. Hawkers bellowed at the top of their voices, desperate to catch the attention of a passer-by.

The market was set up all day and well into the night at weekends. It was where the working class spent their wages after they were paid on a Saturday—assuming it wasn't all given to a greedy landlord or frittered away on booze. As daylight turned to dusk, the area was lit with gaslight, allowing the buyers and sellers alike to benefit from the additional trading hours.

"Can you see Eliza, Raffi?"

"Not yet."

Clarice wondered what an illegal betting operation looked like. With everyone huddled around a myriad of stalls, finding Eliza's felt like a tall order.

"It will definitely be busy. Both businesses are thriving. Joey got the side-line started to make ends meet. He learned the trade from a Chinese bookmaker. I'd never known anyone so flat broke as they were when they started, Joey an orphan and Eliza a divorcee—but now, things are better."

"So, Joey and Eliza are not 'poor' anymore?" Clarice asked.

Not wanting to disclose his clients' information, Raffi gave a diplomatic answer.

"They are reasonably well off for the area."

Saturdays and Sundays brought in the most money at the market. Some of the more monied folks would set out to find the best Sunday lunch available. If their money allowed, the poorer folk grabbed a chunk of bread crust and perhaps a piece of cheese.

"Wednesdays are also busy," Andrew explained. "And Fridays. That's when fresh fish is available. You can hear the sing-song chants of the fishmongers wafting through the air."

"Wednesday is also a good betting day," Raffi added. "No matter what day it is, it's good that we are early, or we would have to queue behind the punters into a bit of outdoor gambling."

"I have never heard of that," said Clarice.

"You are right, lass. There's a reason why Joey
and Eliza's business has been kept hush-
hush."

It was all very confusing for the girl. The only games she
could play were backgammon and chess.

On the lookout for Eliza, Clarice spotted some desperate
souls too impoverished to own a basket, and they tied
all their shopping in their aprons. She'd never seen or
even read about such appalling poverty. She thought
her attempt to live a different life in Chelsea, striving for
a different lifestyle to the elite, she'd achieved a sense of
humility. Realising she was wrong was an incredible
disappointment. She felt like a fraud, still the wealthy
offspring of a rich man.

"For those who could afford them, porters will
carry their purchases," Andrew said. "Mainly
the Irish basketwomen—"

"—who are renowned for drinking and
swearing," Raffi added.

Their antics had her in fits of laughter. She'd never seen
such good-humoured hooliganism in her life. They
behaved as badly as the worst to be found among their
male counterparts. Clarice watched them carry hefty
weights on their backs or heads for those who couldn't
afford a horse or cart. She was in awe. By golly, they
were grafters, thin and wiry yet able to bear
tremendous loads.

"And what about the men, Raffi? Why are they here?"

"Oh, well, if they're not working, they're here to catch up with friends, pop into the barber or secretly sink a pint or place a bet."

"It's a good idea to keep away from the dark alleys," Andrew warned. "There are always pickpockets ready to nab your valuables—"

"There! Come along!" said Raffi, grabbing Clarice's elbow and steering her through the bustling crowd to Eliza O'Shea's stall.

Soon, Clarice was making a beeline forward like a runaway traction engine.

"Stop!" hissed Raffi. "Do your best to look like a housewife, remember. Amble. Peruse. Pick up the merchandise."

"Sorry."

They weaved through the army of women on the move, hunting down all the bargains in their path. Some were accompanied by their children, who nagged and pulled at their skirts. Others were escorted by husbands, eager to tighten the family purse strings, so some money was left for beer.

They reached Eliza's stall. It was definitely popular. Among the crowd of regular punters examining the clothes, young lads were creeping between the stall and the patrons bearing their wares. They reached up, mouths squawking like a cuckoo chick demanding to be fed. A tiny little chap clasped a string of onions in his hand, calling out with a whine to promote the fresh vegetables he had to sell. His wriggling gained him access to nooks, crannies and deals. Clarice wondered if this was how Joey had lived. She decided he must have had quite a talent to capture a shopper's attention in this chaos. How the bets were placed remained a mystery.

Raffi and Andrew escorted Clarice to the front of the jostling throng. Behind the table stood a cheery woman with an easy smile. Everyone knew that Eliza was the sweetheart of the marketplace. With her aura of calm about her, she was the epitome of grace. When she saw Raffi, she winked.

"Raffi, sweetheart! What brings you here? Give me a minute, will you? I'm run off my feet here!"

"Right you are, Eliza. We're not in a rush."

"We?"

"Don't worry, I'll explain."

"What exactly is your relationship with Joey and Eliza?" Clarice asked." You never said?"

"I have their money in safe-keeping, and I pay out the big punters' winnings."

"I suppose that stops anyone wanting to rob the stall, doesn't it? If everyone knows the takings are stored elsewhere, why raid it? What a clever idea."

"Joey's clever idea," added Raffi. "You could say he'd had a premonition that something might happen to him, and he wanted to keep Eliza, the business, and the money away from the wrong hands."

Clarice realised that she was underestimating young Joey. What if he was likely living like a king while she was in fear for his life?

*

Eliza smiled broadly and shook Clarice's hand.

"Joey never mentioned an uncle," she said in a smooth, gentle voice.

"Ah, yes. My father didn't realise he had a nephew until he received the letter from the workhouse."

"Joey's been a real blessing to me. I want him back as much as you do. But I've not seen him since he was taken into care. The only recent thing I've discovered is how much I enjoyed reading about his exploits in the Pall Mall Gazette when he escaped from Slater Street. What will happen to Joey when you find him?"

Her question was a fair one. Clarice knew that O'Shea was afraid to lose Joey. She'd practically raised the boy, and they obviously made a good team.

"I don't have those answers for you, Mrs O'Shea. I can only say that my father is a good man, and he will act in Joey's best interests."

"Thank you," said Eliza, her grace coming to the fore again.

"Mrs O'Shea, have you any inkling where Joey may be?" Clarice asked.

"I assure you I have been to every haunt and bolthole that Joey knew. If I can't find him, nobody else will. I am beginning to think something terrible has hap—."

Her voice broke, and she wiped away a tear, hoping Clarice hadn't seen it fall.

By now, everyone was running out of ideas. How did you find a needle called Joey in a haystack called London's East End?

Raffi and Andrew went to find a few pints, and Clarice and Eliza spent a considerable amount of time lost in polite small talk. Clarice was surprised by Eliza's openness about her past. It saddened her that such a lovely lady was unceremoniously dumped by her husband and replaced with a newer model.

"The real scandal is men can get away with that sort of behaviour. It's time that archaic practices like that were outlawed."

"I don't think you understand, Clarice. Dennis could have had me committed to an asylum. I am grateful to have my freedom. It's not all been rosy. I have had to do a string of unpleasant jobs to take care of myself. Until little Joey came into my life, I suppose I was at a stalemate. Neither free nor trapped. His enthusiasm gave me an incentive to try something new. I mean, there are some shortcomings in our business dealings. mainly that it's illegal," she added with a grin. "But there is always a new day, always something better on the horizon. There's hope."

Clarice liked the woman. She had courage.

"If we find Joey before you do, I will send a message via Raffi," Clarice told her.

"Thank you, my dear. I appreciate your concern."

Raffi and Andrew returned to the stall. There was no more urgency to their journey, and they slowed their pace, giving Clarice another opportunity to examine what went on around her. Maybe one of these people knew where Joey was? Could one of them be hiding him? Who knew?

The heart of the market had to be the costermongers, with their wares neatly stacked on wheeled carts. Their 'barra boys' helped by pushing the wheelbarrows laden with goods for sale. Costers sold provisions in the street, but some also had stationary stalls. Many of these itinerant folk travelled two to ten miles a day. Clarice found them interesting, with their peculiar language not understood by many.

"They speak another language, don't they, Andrew?" Clarice said. "I can't fathom it."

He laughed.

"Indeed, they do, lass. And don't try to work it out either. They are too quick for that. Some of them might pronounce words backwards. For example, 'Cool the esilop' would mean, 'Look the police' to the knowing ear. If they can sense you catching on, they'll just use a different technique to disguise what they mean, and you'll be stumped again."

The flower girls darted behind the shoppers' heels, shouting rhymes about the blooms they held, hoping to sell a little cheer to their impoverished community. Their pervasive calls could be heard throughout Spitalfields.

'Please, kind lady, buy my violets. Poor little girl! Oh, do, please, buy a bunch!'

The place was like another world—a world Clarice was determined to immerse herself in.

21

THE LECTURE

Clarice stood in a great exhibition hall at the British Museum as if she was a mountain explorer lost in thick fog. She had a ticket with a seat number, but she was flustered and couldn't find it. There was a hubbub of people around her. It was like the world was spinning around her head, and she was slipping into a deep hypnotic trance. What she would give for a cool glass of water and sit down for a moment. She made her way to the table where drinks were served and had a refreshing glass of lemonade. The instant the sharpness hit her tongue, she felt better. She took a deep breath, opened her small purse, and found the ticket nestled within it.

Miss Lawrence made a beguiling subject and turned a lot of male heads. Her hair was a mess of curls, her hat looked crushed, and her clothes were an unmatched riot of colour. Her dress code resembled nothing that was currently fashionable. There was a freedom about her that men found enticing. Perhaps they sensed the confidence required to live an unorthodox lifestyle. Furthermore, she was simply beautiful, giving the appearance of softness and warmth. Men usually identified this countenance as welcoming. They soon found out they were mistaken.

Also in the audience was Thomas McGill, still seething at being cast off by Clarice on the way to Slater Street Workhouse. On the one hand, he was humiliated. On the other, his fantasies of how he would repay her snub drove his pursuit. For him, it was definitely bittersweet. Knowing running out of a public event would be far more tricky than fleeing a cab, he pulled a few strings and wangled a seat next to her.

Clarice acknowledged her peers and sat down. The lights dimmed. Just before the lecture started, she saw a man wending his way down her aisle. *'Not him! Not that seat?'*.

"What a coincidence to be alongside you. You look as lovely as ever, my dear," he purred.

There was that word again. *'Dear.'*

Professor Abercrombie walked towards the podium and introduced the guest speaker. The priceless Assyrian tablet had pride of place on a large oak table to the left of the stage. The carving looked heavy, and it was. Moving it anywhere took great effort and was best attempted with a small crew.

"Ladies and gentlemen, the marks on this stone are more than mere scratches. They are deep, deliberate shapes and patterns, a language that only a handful of scholars can decipher. I'm sure you'll agree it is an honour for any scholar of ancient history to be in the same room as this article and to be able to inspect it at such close proximity."

A hush fell in the room as the audience adored the exquisite object.

"To talk us through this magnificent piece is a visiting academic from Harvard, Professor Jack Wyatt. When it comes to Ashuri cuneiform alphabets, he is recognised as the world's leading scholar of this generation. He has received praise from the President of the United States himself for deciphering the script. The professor is also the author of two highly respected volumes, both relating to the Assyrian culture."

Abercrombie wandered across to Raubach, and the two of them disappeared.

The polite applause coaxed a figure from the wings. The archaeologist was tall and lanky, with sun-bleached blonde hair and amber skin from spending day after day digging in the hot Middle Eastern sun. His smile at the audience was both confident and sincere. With piercing blue eyes, he scoured the room and its occupants. Suddenly they halted on Clarice. He felt compelled to stare at her, not just because of her magnetic beauty but also because she was strangely familiar. *'Where do I know you from?'* He hoped the answer would come to him if he stared at her long enough.

Equally, Clarice wondered if he was the drunken man with the cap in the police station, but she couldn't be sure. Now that he was sober, clean-shaven, and respectable, he was hard to identify.

"I am Professor Jack Wyatt," he said without taking his eyes off of Clarice.

For the first time in his life, Jack Wyatt was speechless. He didn't know what he was doing or why he was there. Dumbstruck was the correct word to describe his circumstances.

He forced himself to tear his eyes away from Clarice. He didn't dare look at her for the rest of the lecture— unable to trust himself to remain focused. Clarice didn't hear a single word of Thomas McGill's crass whispering in her ear. She clung to the professor's every word, captivated by his academic prowess—and dashing figure.

The audience had an opportunity to ask questions. There was a slew of highly technical and intelligent points made. When the last question was answered, Clarice slowly put up her hand. Her first question pertained to the cuneiform. Their eyes met as he answered it. The air almost crackled.

"Is that everything?"

"Almost. How long will you be staying in London?"

"That depends on who's asking, ma'am," he joked in his Yankee drawl. "What is your name?"

"Miss Lawrence."

The professor answered professionally, although his cheeks turned cherry red.

"I will be in London for as long as I am needed, miss."

Most of the audience deemed the reply to be practical, but Miss Lawrence appreciated the ambiguity meant just for her.

*

There was a great deal of excitement after Jack Wyatt finished his lecture. The group's interest in the tablet soon waned. It was the professor they were most interested in. Soon he was surrounded by admirers wanting to prove their intelligence. It had been a long day, and he was tired of the questions, but the crowd refused to disperse. A head and shoulders above the throng, he scoured the room, desperate to catch a glimpse of Clarice.

The confusion after the talk was the perfect opportunity for Abercrombie, Raubach, and a couple of stooges masquerading as couriers to slip the tablet away to the East India Dock.

*

Elsewhere in the room, another eagle-eyed person stood in the shadows, observing everyone like a hawk, ready to strike should anyone dare move or touch anything in his domain.

Malcolm Featherstone's mind couldn't rest. Not only was there an intruder concealed somewhere within the confines of his beloved museum, but there was a large crowd of inept dignitaries flooding into one of the most prestigious display rooms in the building. He watched as someone laughed a little too loudly to be sober. The bitter custodian loathed them all, happy to turn the beloved British Museum into a circus.

Mr Featherstone watched a history professor steer a young woman through a connecting door towards the large Jacobean bed, eager to give the lovely lady something to think about. He went to great lengths to explain the intricacies of the piece to her and took great pleasure in opening the secret panel. To his astonishment, he looked into the face of a young boy. Poor little Joey's eyes were the size of saucers. He knew that a man of his class wouldn't look the other way and show him mercy.

"Well, Malcolm, it seems we have a rat in the bed—in the form of a boy."

The historian moved out of the way to give the apoplectic custodian a better view.

Featherstone looked vicious as he strode over, arms reaching forward, eyes narrowed, ready to throttle the living daylights out of the trespasser.

Surrounded, Joey was trapped. There would be no running away from this predicament.

"Get out at once!" Mr Featherstone bellowed.

The whole room had come to a standstill.

Joey emerged, blinking. Onlookers noted the grubby little lad was wearing an old tailcoat and had a battered top hat in his hand.

Mr Featherstone grabbed him by the ear and marched him towards the door.

"Leave me alone," shouted Joey. "You're ripping my ears off, I tell ya!"

The pompous Professor Abercrombie met Mr Featherstone halfway across the room.

"And this? What on earth are you doing, Featherstone? What's all the ruckus for? Tonight, of all nights!"

Featherstone lectured him.

"This little oik has been living in the museum for days. I told you that there was someone here who shouldn't be. I bet you believe me now, though, eh, Paul?"

Abercrombie's face was flushed from embarrassment as he growled at Malcolm.

"We'll discuss this later, Featherstone. For now, get him out of here,"

The custodian dragged his quarry towards the exit.

"Leave me alone," yelled Joey. "You're hurting me. Let me go!"

"If you promise to behave and tell me your name, I'll think about it."

"Joey, sir."

"Joey, what?"

"Cornish, sir"

Clarice Lawrence had been watching the scene unfold from across the room. When she heard the name, she sprang into action. As Featherstone dragged the child out of the room, Clarice followed.

Professor Jack Wyatt had watched the debacle from his high vantage point. When he caught sight of Clarice running towards the door, he excused himself and followed her. He wanted to know who she was—and why she was prepared to defend the boy.

Joey stood in the middle of a group of watchmen, and Mr Featherstone refused to let go of his ear. Clarice pushed her way through the men until she stood face to face with the custodian.

"Sir, I know that boy," she told him.

Joey looked at Clarice. He'd never seen her before.

"How do you know him, Miss?"

"He is my cousin and has been lost for some time."

Joey didn't utter a sound, wondering what was happening. He didn't have any family, let alone a long-lost cousin. Jack Wyatt, equally confused, barged his way towards Clarice. Featherstone was now goggle-eyed with rage.

"He is not a distant cousin. He is an intruder, a vagabond, and a thief,"

"I will take responsibility for him now," Clarice said.

"You will not. He's going to the police station, and then he will be going to gaol. Get out of my way."

The watchmen closed ranks, forming a human wall. Any hope Clarice had to snatch the boy to safety evaporated.

A triumphant Malcolm Featherstone didn't give the police the opportunity to throw Joey into the Black Maria. He did it himself.

Everything happened so fast that Clarice was dizzy. She forced her way out on the street, looked around and hailed a cab. As she got in, she felt a pair of hands push her. A man climbed in—Jack Wyatt.

"What? Why are you here?"

Suddenly, the other cab door was ripped open, and another person appeared—Thomas McGill.

"I thought you may need some help, Clarice," McGill cooed.

"Is this your brother, Clarice?" asked Jack.

"No, he most certainly isn't! He's a—he's a friend of my father's."

Thomas McGill was the last person she wanted to see, but she didn't want to argue with him in front of Jack.

The cab bumped over the cobbles. Clarice and Jack sat shoulder to shoulder. She turned her head slightly to look up at him. He looked down and smiled. Jack Wyatt was in his element. He hated a dull moment.

*

It was the same inspector from a week ago. He looked at Clarice and Jack.

"That boy, Joey Cornish, we are here to bail him out," said Jack.

"Professor Wyatt, how nice to see you again," the officer joked.

The police station was in pandemonium. Mr Featherstone refused to let go of Joey. Joey was screaming blue murder. He was afraid for the first time in his life, remembering what fellow orphan Alfie had told him about prison life.

Thomas McGill stood in the background, observing the chaos. He couldn't tear his eyes off the beautiful, passionate Clarice. It irked him that Professor Wyatt had usurped him and become her protector.

Joey was acting out the wildest tantrum of his life. His mouth was wide open, and he was still yelling.

Suddenly, Joey turned around and kicked Mr Featherstone in the shins. Featherstone dropped onto his haunches, desperate to rub his throbbing leg. Joey was fast, and his escape unexpected. Using the crowd dodging skills honed in the market, he slipped through the crowd and out of the station.

Joey Tophat had escaped—again!

Jack grabbed Clarice's hand. Together, they crashed out onto the street, then blundered about blindly searching for the lad, but he was gone. They stopped to take a breath.

"We need to slow down," said Jack. "We'll never find him if we run about like lunatics."

"I have to find him. He's an orphan in my father's care. It's my job—my duty— to take him home."

Jack looked down at her and smiled. He brushed a piece of her unruly hair from her face and tucked it behind her ear. There was compassion in his eyes and smile.

"It's alright. I understand. Now, where would you go if you were Joey, Clarice?"

"Eliza O'Shea."

"Was she his guardian?"

"Ish. Mentor and business partner."

"Business partner? What does Joey do for a living? He's a kid."

"Together, they run one of the largest underground bookies in Spitalfields. Quick. Let's go before McGill follows us."

Jack put his head back and laughed. It was proving to be one of his better evenings in London.

Clarice felt as if she and Jack had been friends all their lives. She didn't want to take her hand from his or wriggle away. She didn't feel the same nauseating dread she did in the company of Thomas.

"This isn't your matter," Clarice shouted while Jack tugged her along.

"I know. I could be drinking," he clowned.

"Why are you doing this, Jack?"

"Because it's an adventure."

There was no sign of Joey. All they could do was hope to find Eliza.

"I have a vague idea. I met her recently, and we chatted. If we really struggle, I can try Raffi Fischer's place in the morning. He'll know."

Although finding Eliza's tiny abodc in Shoreditch would be challenging, Clarice was confident that Joey would be there.

*

Clarice and Jack had enjoyed the moment of euphoria that their escapade brought them until they realised where they were. For outsiders, Whitechapel's streets were treacherous at night. Some parts were off-limits even to the police patrolling in groups.

They pushed on, asking a few street sellers for directions to the likely location. There couldn't be too many pleasant streets in such a hellhole. Thankfully, Eliza was well known, and soon they were on the right track. The standard of housing was definitely more salubrious. The dwellings had doors for one thing.

"This one, do you think, Jack? 27?"

He nodded and knocked on the door quietly.

There was movement inside—footsteps. Then a woman's voice called out.

"Who's there?"

"It's Clarice, Mrs O'Shea."

The door swung open. Eliza wasn't smiling. Far from it. She looked concerned.

"I'm terribly sorry for calling at such a late hour, but I have news of Joey."

"So, do I. You'd better come in."

On a fireside chair sat the boy.

"Joey," said Eliza, "this is Miss Lawrence, who I told you about."

"I know. She's been stalking me."

"Not stalking, Joey, I promise!"

Joey studied Clarice and then Jack.

"If you try and take me away from Eliza, I'll run away, and you'll never find me again."

"I won't take you anywhere you don't want to go. I am your cousin, not your keeper."

Joey eyed her, not sure whether to trust her. Silence reigned.

"There is a problem greater than Joey," Eliza said. "Tell them what you told me."

Joey went into detail about overhearing Professor Abercrombie and Raubach discussing the stone. Jack's face fell.

"Are you sure?" Jack asked. "If you are lying, it can cause a lot of unnecessary trouble."

"I don't cheat or lie. Anyone round here would tell you."

Eliza nodded in agreement.

"Well, I am glad to hear that. What made you go to the museum to begin with?"

"I needed somewhere to lay low after fleeing the workhouse. I wasn't going under no railway arch. I just slipped in through one of the side doors. Quite cosy it was."

"Tell me more," Jack said.

"They intend to lose it. Fudge the paperwork when it's in transit. Then it will end up at some posh prince's place."

"You must tell the police, Joey. That stone is priceless. We have a duty to protect it. If a private collector hides it away—well, I dread to think."

"I'm not going near the police, Jack," answered Joey. "They'll nick me for running away."

Jack was frustrated; the little fellow was more stubborn and smarter than he'd given him credit for.

"Alright. How about this. You come with me and tell the story to the ambassador. Let him handle it rather than the police?"

"S'pose."

"Good lad. I knew that conscience of yours would kick in," Jack said with pride. "At this time of night, he will be at his club on Regent Street. Come on. We will take a cab."

"Not on your own," said Eliza, darting to block the doorway.

"And I am coming, too," Clarice added.

"Well, it looks like that's settled," said Jack, buttoning up his coat. "We've either turned into a committee or an angry mob. Everyone ready?"

Joey put on his top hat.

"I am now," he said, and they left the building together.

22

THE GENTLEMEN'S CLUB

The cab driver was astounded when Jack pointed him to Regent Street and gave him the name of one of the most expensive clubs in the city. He looked at the two women, then at Joey, and shook his head. *'There was no way they'll all be getting in.'*

Upper-class men in London regarded the gentlemen's clubs very much as the centre of their world and the foundation of their social lives. The upper- and upper-middle-class men loved to spend much of their time and money hidden from their families while in grand surroundings. No two clubs were the same; each had a distinct style and peculiar offerings and characteristics.

The St. Thomas Club catered for academics, politicians, ambassadors and diplomats. This was where the real decisions were made. The Houses of Parliament were just large, airy old halls where they gathered to sign the documents.

America's ambassador, Kyle O'Rourke, loved the place. It was his second home. He found everything he'd come to expect at his regular residence, except his wife and six children, who exhausted him. He preferred to spend as many evenings as possible residing at the club under the auspices of business.

Kyle stopped short of using the club address for official documentation, mailings, and appointments. He didn't dare entrust documents to the care of others. Gossip abounded but was referred to as healthy communication and sharing of information among members. Leaked information would travel far and wide. Sometimes that was helpful, other times not.

Although it was known as a place for the learned, no one knew that the German Consul had invited visiting professor Heinrich Raubach to take in the facilities.

The American ambassador had cringed when he'd brought Jack Wyatt to the club. The man had no social boundaries. It wasn't that he didn't know what the social boundaries were—he just refused to keep to them. Kyle wondered how Jack had ever been appointed to Harvard with his terrible attitude, and he also couldn't understand why the man had no desire to climb the social ladder. The answer was simple. Jack hated stuffy old clubs. He preferred the rough and tumble of pubs. In the club, masculinity was established by job title and the choice of single malt. He had no need to prove anything. He enjoyed storytelling, joking, and banter among the men—real men. He was the type of fellow who enjoyed getting his hands dirty on a dig, not ordering people about from the side of the trench.

The cab stopped outside of the glossy black doors of the club.

"You stay here. No clever capers. Let me do this. Understood?"

They nodded, not sure they could keep to their word.

Joey was the first to fold.

"I am coming with you, and I'm not prepared to argue."

The concierge greeted the curious strangers on the marble steps.

"Professor Jack Wyatt. I'm a visiting professor affiliated with the American Embassy. I'm with Ambassador O'Rourke. Kyle?"

"Welcome, professor."

The concierge looked from Jack to Joey, who was still wearing the top hat.

Jack leaned forward and whispered behind his hand:

"He's a dwarf. Very sensitive about it too. Don't kick up a fuss, please."

"As long as the midget behaves himself," the concierge said, looking down his nose at Joey.

The concierge was convinced he'd seen the rumpus Wyatt inebriated on his last visit but let them in anyway, not wanting to cause a scene in public. He popped his head inside and looked at the doorman. He pointed two fingers towards his beady eyes and then jabbed a finger in Jack and Joey's direction. His colleague nodded.

Instantly, Jack hated the place as much as his first visit, the home of pompous greying aristocrats and politicians, ruthless military men and greedy industrialists. Even the young ones with no real careers irritated him. So many of the newly graduated men fresh from out-of-town would often live at their club in London for two or three years, renting a room until they got to know the city and had the financial means to buy a house or flat.

Professor Paul Abercrombie was one such young man, except he'd never left the club. Having grown up in Northumberland, he had moved to London after completing his education at Oxford and took up residence at St Thomas's. A typical day would see Abercrombie dine at the club, taking his breakfast and supper there, only leaving the place to go to work. He always had a perfunctory nod ready for everyone. He loved ingratiating himself, hoping it would advance his status among the members. Having found his feet, he'd learned to understand the ways of London and its people. Next, he spent a great deal of his time meeting foreigners who would nudge his career forward irrespective of how mediocre his knowledge was. He took to shaking hands and making new acquaintances. He learned to play billiards and chess, although he had no understanding of the strategic angles of either game. He spent his time in the bar, looking for opportunities as he wrote notes, quoted regurgitated philosophy and imbibed copious amounts of coffee.

Thomas McGill was cut from the same cloth, wishy-washy and self-interested. In his father's home, almost every need could be satisfied. The only thing it lacked was privacy. The McGill family had their lives on display and their goings-on plastered across the society columns in the national newspapers. They used their home to entertain guests, hosting parties, dinners, formal teas, and other evenings of entertainment. Within the gentlemen's club walls, Thomas could escape protocol and his parents. He'd even schmoozed his father to pay the annual fees.

Jack found a seat facing into a quiet corner. He manhandled Joey into it.

> "You—sit down here and do not move your
> rump off the chair until I return. Understand?
> This isn't a game. If Abercrombie or Raubach
> spots you, you'll be for the high jump."

Joey nodded, and then Jack went from room to room, searching for O'Rourke.

Wyatt found the ambassador in one of the many lounges and explained the ruse to steal the stone. O'Rourke exploded into a stream of expletives, calling the two crooked professors every name under the sun. It was hardly the dignified and grateful response Jack Wyatt expected. Heads were beginning to turn.

"How dare those two think they can get one over on the good old US of A. We'll put an end to this little plan. Meddling fools."

"You're the fool, Kyle, shouting like that. I bet they know we're onto them now. The stone is as good as lost already."

Frantic, the ambassador knocked his bourbon back in one go, and then he clicked his fingers at a passing waiter.

"Another one in there. And make it a double."

Kyle was so eager to have a quick hit of liquor that lots of the precious golden liquid dribbled down the side of his mouth and onto his black dinner jacket. He looked a mess. Then he started swearing again. Jack tried to restrain his colleague, talk some sense into him, and get him to be more tactful. Alas, it quickly developed into a tussle and then a full-blown struggle, with the two grown men rolling on the floor.

"Let me at them," growled a drunken Kyle,
with Jack sat astride him, pinning him down
by the wrists.

In the wings was Thomas McGill, watching the American contingent make utter fools of themselves. It was this kind of coarse, ungentlemanly behaviour that the British abhorred. He was delighted.

More delightful still was that it was his new nemesis, Wyatt, discrediting himself in front of the entire club. After her question, only someone with a swinging brick for a heart would have failed to pick up on the attraction between Jack and Clarice. This appalling public display would surely take the brawling professor out of the running and make him seem a more suitable candidate for a clandestine affair. Thomas chuckled to himself at the thought.

*

In the cocktail lounge, Professors Abercrombie and Raubach were in deep conversation.

"Has the crate been shipped yet, Paul?"

"Yes, it has. Our friend at the harbour is
altering the manifest as we speak. It will reach
Germany within the next week."

"I plan to go back and spend a bit more time
with that girl, Violet. Perhaps spend some of
that money and buy her outright from

Madame du Puy. Hole her up in a little room somewhere. Get the doctor to give her a clean bill of health, and then it's all systems go, as they say. Now that she's been used, I'll get her for a knockdown rate."

Abercrombie made a low guttural sound in agreement.

Unaware that the cat was out of the bag about their little scheme, the two academics left the lounge and strolled out onto the landing. Thomas McGill remained to watch Ambassador O'Rourke behave like a hooligan. The more information he had, the more influence he could exert over Martha Lawrence and get her to force Clarice to comply with his physical demands.

*

It was the battered top hat that exposed Joey. The outline was unmistakable, and Professors Abercrombie and Raubach saw it simultaneously. Paul nudged his partner and motioned for him to follow. Left alone in the quiet corner, Joey had fallen asleep in the soft, warm chair. The Geordie grabbed the boy roughly and put his large hand around his scrawny throat. Joey woke up with a lurch. He felt a warm whisper in his ear.

"Shut up. Alright? Else, I will throttle you if you utter a sound."

The two men had not expected to be interrupted. A gentle cough was enough to fluster them. Abercrombie loosened his grip on Joey's throat and jumped back, while Raubach behaved nonchalantly and gazed out of a window and looked down at the street.

"I will take care of the boy," Thomas McGill said abruptly.

"How dare you!" snarled Abercrombie.

"I have a lot of influence in this club, Paul. Consider yourself blackballed. Pack your bags and leave, or I will expose you as a child molester."

Abercrombie was shocked but knew that he was snookered. He turned to leave, announcing he would resign from St Thomas the following morning.

"Are you taking me back to Clarice, sir?" said Joey's little face, looking up.

"Something like that."

*

Wyatt had lost all patience with O'Rourke. As usual, Jack took matters into his own hands. He searched high and low for Abercrombie, but he had vanished. A servant told the American the man had retired to his room.

"Thank you. You've been most helpful."

Wyatt crashed into Abercrombie's room without knocking.

"Where have you sent the tablet to?"

Paul said nothing.

Jack grabbed Abercrombie by the lapels and gave him a good shake.

"Squeal! Now!"

"The East India Company Docks. It's on the Witten Paarden, a steamer heading for Germany."

"You'd better be telling the truth, Paul, or I will be back for you."

But it wouldn't be Jack who came back. It would be the police. As soon as he had the tablet and the forged paperwork back in his possession, the next stop would be the station.

*

After Abercrombie had received his marching orders from McGill, Heinrich had gone for a long walk through the streets. Thomas grabbed Joey by the neck and marched him downstairs.

"Act normal if you know what's good for you, sonny."

"But I'm supposed to be waiting for Professor Wyatt."

McGill gave the boy's neck an eyewatering pinch.

"Never mind him. How did you give the police the slip and get here, boy?"

"I sneaked out of the cop shop and went to see Mrs O'Shea. She looked after me before they sent me to the workhouse. Then I got a cab with her, Mr Jack and Miss Lawrence. The ladies are still in the cab waiting for us."

"Are they?"

It was all working out for McGill. Clarice Lawrence would be delighted to see her lad back, and it was Thomas who had rescued him—not the Yank.

Joey showed Thomas where the cab was parked. The boy was relieved to get a shove inside and tumble on the floor between Eliza and Clarice.

"Gosh, am I pleased to see you!"

Mrs O'Shea plucked the boy up and hugged him so hard his eyes nearly popped out. He hid his head on her shoulder.

"I am in frightful trouble, Eliza," he mumbled,

"You're not in trouble, Joey. You were forced into the workhouse against your will. Wanting to escape was entirely reasonable. The authorities will listen. Especially now you have a family. If anything, they'll be glad they don't have to pay for your bed and board."

Joey gave a weak laugh as he raised his face to look at her.

"My father is a good man," Clarice assured
him. "He will respect your wishes."

All the fussing around the boy put McGill's nose out of joint.

"You should show more gratitude towards
me, Clarice," Thomas sneered.

"Yes, of course. Thank you very much."

Thomas was temporarily appeased. He lost his smugness when Jack ran out of the club, pushed him aside, and climbed into the cab.

"East India Docks—now!" he yelled to the
driver, "and get there fast, my man. There will
be a reward in it for you!"

The whip cracked on the horse's back, and the carriage seemed to shoot off faster than The Flying Scotsman. Thomas tried to haul himself inside, but it was too late. The cab had gone.

*

The carriage thundered towards the Thames. The mist was hovering on the water, and there was a slight frosty breeze. Progress was swift initially, but the closer they came to the harbour, the busier it became. The wharves were lit with gas lamps, and Clarice could see them loading the great ships. The East India Company harbour never slept. The docks were buzzing with merchants, chandlers, restaurants, and taverns. It was the most stunning quayside in Britain.

Jack regretted dragging the whole entourage with him. Carrying the extra passengers slowed progress. Worse, it took some time to locate the Witten Paarden. It would have been easier if he were by himself rather than part of a search party.

"Driver. Stop here, please, but wait. I'll be back."

Jack leapt out of the cab as it slowed with Clarice close on his heel. By the time they reached the mooring, the gangplank had been lifted. Slowly, the ship moved from its berth. Wyatt jumped, waved his arms wildly, and shouted like a foghorn.

"Oi! Hey! Stop the ship!"

Nobody paid any attention onboard the vessel, and the quayside onlookers wondered what all the fuss was about. A young lovestruck couple approached.

"They won't stop now," the man told him.
"Whatever you have on it has already left."

Jack cursed loudly and more impressively than the Irish hawkers in Spitalfields Market. Joey caught up with them and cursed like a docker too.

23

THE BALL

At the embassy, there was a heated argument about whose fault it was that the stone was pinched from under their noses. The blundering ambassador had offered an olive branch to Wyatt.

"Please, you must attend a lavish ball that the McGills are hosting. All the members of high society will be there."

It sounded awfully stuffy to Wyatt and not a 'treat' at all. O'Rourke wasn't taking no for an answer.

"We need to build a few bridges after our altercation in the club. Show we are not savages from across the pond."

"Alright. You win, Kyle. I'll go. But there are conditions."

"Which are?" said O'Rourke wincing.

"My ticket will be a plus one, and I get to choose my guest."

"Very well. Just don't turn up with some wild and uncouth fishwife."

Jack Wyatt wanted to punch O'Rourke but refrained. It was a rare occasion when his head overruled his heart.

"Will Miss Lawrence meet your exacting standards?"

"Of course. Clarice is hardly common, is she? And Frank is a fine, upstanding man. I met him in Washington."

The ambassador thought his response would satisfy Wyatt, but he was wrong. The demands kept coming.

"Also, Ms Eliza O'Shea is to attend—with a guest. Master Cornish."

"Out of the question. I can't tell the McGills whom to invite to their own party. What has got into you lately?"

The ambassador shook his head in frustration, wishing he'd never suggested Jack Wyatt share his knowledge with the elite of London. His goodwill and desire to improve foreign relations had become a thorn in his side.

"May I ask why you are so insistent?"

"Have you forgotten Master Cornish has exposed a criminal gang in the midst of the academic world? Recovering the stone would be impossible without his information. It's the least you can do."

O'Rourke said nothing.

"I suggest you have a chat with Lord McGill at St Thomas's. Soften him up with a few cognacs. A man of your standing can pull a few strings, surely."

*

It was the first ball Clarice Lawrence had attended in years, and she'd only accepted the invitation for one reason—Jack Wyatt. Even then, she'd taken quite a bit of persuasion.

"Please come with me," Jack pleaded. "I won't get through the night without you. You know I don't do hoity-toity."

"No. Definitely not. May I leave if I am unhappy?"

"Only if you take me with you," Jack hooted, but he was also serious behind the mask of humour.

Their adventures had forged a deep bond in his heart for her. Authentic and independent, he never felt uncomfortable with her. He never had to pretend like he had to with other women he'd met before. He could just be himself, and in a world where everyone else wanted to constrain and pigeonhole him, she was his lifeline.

*

The event of the year was to be held in the private home of Lord and Lady McGill, hosted in honour of the British Historical Society. The topic for discussion was supposed to be the stone, but that had to be changed. There was talk of unwrapping a mummy instead.

"I noted that your daughter Clarice will be attending the ball with Professor Jack Wyatt," muttered Lady McGill as she read the guest list to Martha.

"Is she? That's news to me," grizzled Martha.

Martha was bitterly disappointed that a brawling American was escorting her only daughter to such a prestigious ball and not someone more suitable, like Thomas. Equally, Lady McGill felt her family had dodged a bullet.

"Do you think Clarice will be more demure than usual? I don't expect her character to change very much, but perhaps her attire could be toned down a little."

"I shall send a note, Prudence. Then it is in writing she is expected to dress appropriately."

"I appreciate that gesture. Thank you."

Martha didn't. She was tired of the blatant criticism. This time it made her uncomfortable. For the first time, she looked at her friend with daggers in her eyes. Lady

McGill never looked anyone in the eye, and thus, Martha's annoyance went unseen.

'I'll teach you. I won't send the stupid note. It wouldn't make a blind bit of difference anyway.'

Martha was tired of taking responsibility for Clarice's disdain for what was expected of a young lady. She'd given Clarice lectures on etiquette. She'd bought her books on how to dress appropriately, what to say in specific situations, which cutlery to use first, and how to curtsey.

Her daughter was neither common nor crass. She never intended to create a spectacle for the sake of it. She was polite, respectful and well-spoken. What she did rebel against were pointless social expectations. She avoided petty people. She was more cerebral than social. It dawned on her that Thomas McGill was shallow, selfish and spoilt—everything Clarice was not.

Protocols ruled Lady McGill's life. 'The Ballroom Guide' gave advice on how to create an invitation list to a private ball, and the lady of the house followed the manual to the letter. One piece of advice was to invite a few more people than could comfortably be accommodated so that absences would go unnoticed. She would invite more men than ladies to ensure that the sprung wooden dance floor was filled. She breathed a sigh of relief when Thomas had told her he wasn't taking a partner. *'At last, he'll have the opportunity to meet other young women, dainty debutantes, far more acceptable than Clarice. This silly obsession of his will soon fizzle out.'*

Lady McGill spent many weeks, and more money than she could afford, to ensure her ball would be talked about for years to come. She was like a Tudor aristocrat planning for a royal progress visit. Nothing was too ostentatious. Nothing was too much trouble. She even considered extending one of the wings to her gigantic London home. The head of the household was close to breaking point as the to-do list grew far faster than it shrank.

"Dawson! There you are. How are the ballroom decorations coming along? I want it to be resplendent for our distinguished guests!"

"Yes, ma'am. Wonderfully, ma'am. If you'll excuse me, I'm overseeing the cleaning of the chandeliers."

"Good. Oh, and Dawson, remember to ask Mrs McKay to dust the top of the picture frames. I don't want another disaster like last time. People notice the little details."

"Yes, ma'am."

"I can't wait to see the ladies' stunning gowns. They always look beautiful, their elegant outfits enhancing the rich décor, don't you

think, Martha? —Martha? —Are you
listening?"

In truth, Martha had given up listening to the endless
preparations long ago.

*

Few people in London got to know the real Professor
Jack Wyatt, but his head-turning good looks meant
many women knew of him. Some were more discreet
than others. Quite a few gawped at him, transfixed. Even
Martha Lawrence was impressed.

On the night of the ball, Jack Wyatt had chosen to don a
stylish black suit. He lacked a tailcoat, for him irksome
and old-fashioned. However, his shirt collar was
starched to crisp perfection and his white tie perfectly
knotted. His patent black leather shoes shone like
mirrors. His hair was neatly styled, and his face
perfectly clean-shaven. Jack Wyatt was the most well-
turned-out and handsome man in the room.

More surprising, and to many irritating, was the woman
on his arm. Rather than wear the expected light-
coloured ball gown, she had chosen a darker dress, set
off with a delicate sapphire necklace. The plunging
neckline was revealing and exposed her seductive
shoulders. The peacock blue fabric accentuated her
amber skin. A soft silk stole draped over her arm,
beautifully embroidered and edged with a delicate gold
fringe. Her feather-light silk gloves reached her elbows.

She didn't carry a fan to send secret messages to would-be suitors and refused a dance card. She had no intention of dancing with anyone. She had styled her hair in a loose bun, pinned up with exquisite ivory combs, but several tresses had broken free, softening the look. Her ensemble would be the talk of the town.

Eliza O'Shea caused a stir when she arrived, but the gasps were for a different reason—being discarded and divorced by her husband.

Joey Cornish had thrown away his tattered tails, the Lawrences funding a new outfit for him. One item was out of place—the battered top hat. Something about that hat gave him security, and he refused to wear or buy a new one. No matter how Eliza tried to coax and bribe him, Joey flatly refused to relinquish his old hat.

Behind her back, the cruel gossips discussed Clarice's outfit. She could hear the whispers but chose to ignore them. Martha wasn't so lucky. She braced herself for another one of Prudence's tongue-lashings about breaches in protocol. Lady McGill pulled up her nose and prepared to strike.

> "Thank goodness Clarice wasn't escorted by Thomas. He would have been the laughingstock of London. Your daughter has done it again. She looks positively out of place here."

Martha's body stiffened.

"She is unchaperoned as well-"

Frank Lawrence heard the comment and was ready to retaliate, but Martha replied first.

"Please, just shut up, Prudence. Clarice has no interest in Thomas. She is devoted to her studies."

"—And that brash brawling American, if the stories are to be believed. Why Lord McGill agreed to give him a ticket remains a mystery."

Martha took Frank's arm.

"Come, my dear, let's go and listen to the string quartet. They have such talent."

*

Thomas McGill was living in fear of his mother and never left the ballroom once. He deliberately ignored several of the most attractive girls. They sat demurely, awaiting his attention if he deemed them beautiful enough, and he loved to crush their confidence. He had invited some young ladies to dance, but they never got his full attention because his eye was caught by Clarice standing by the far wall.

One protocol McGill wasn't prepared to breach in such important company was approaching Clarice before she acknowledged him—and that might take some time with Jack Wyatt on the prowl. Eventually, there was nothing for it but to walk over. At least it would be easier than stalking her around Chelsea's coffee shops.

"You look different but still magnificent," he blundered. "Would you like to dance?"

His forefinger stroked her arm under the stole. Clarice had felt the touch of Thomas's soft sweaty hands once before, and she couldn't bear the thought of them pawing at her again. She politely declined, but the moody young man persisted.

"Thomas, let me be clear. I know you have no intention of marrying me, and I have no intention of ever being in your bed in any sort of temporary arrangement or whatever you have in mind. I think that brings this little chapter in our lives to a close. Yes?"

The comments were as direct as she could make them. Thomas wasn't heartbroken—he was humiliated. Clarice should have been a notch on his bedpost, taught a lesson for spurning his advances. He made a slight bow and slowly moved to the other side of the room, plotting and scheming as he went.

From the corner of his eye, he saw his mother's disappointed face, which never ended well for him. It looked like she was threatening to walk over, so he paced over to a very plain girl sitting alone on the far side of the ballroom. Her mother lurked a few paces away, keeping tabs on her offspring. The parents always loved to interfere when a family had few marital options and wanted to marry up the social pecking order, not down. Thomas McGill asked the shy girl to dance. Her mother gave a slight nod in agreement. Fuelled with spite from Clarice's rejection, he would coax the girl into a false sense of security. He would charm her, make sure her cocktail glass was never empty. By the end of the night, in some dusty annexe room, she would have been thoroughly used.

*

Jack Wyatt walked towards Clarice and took her arm.

"Can I interest you in a gallop around the room?"

Clarice began to laugh.

"Neigh. But thank you, Jack."

Jack squeezed her arm ever so slightly and looked into her eyes for a second too long. Clarice sensed the tension between them was escalating, just as it had been since they met.

*

The day that Lord O'Shea divorced Lizelle, he was assured that she would never be allowed to attend an event like this. His friends agreed to close ranks and make sure she was excluded—permanently. That explained his mortified expression when he saw her arrive with a young boy of all people.

He gritted his teeth and looked at his delightful second wife, as delicate as the bloom on an orchid. He didn't know if she could weather the scandal that the situation would create.

In retrospect, he was sorry that he'd married Ella Sinclair. It was a case of his loins over his brain. They were hopelessly unsuited. He was a big boorish bully of a politician. She was highly strung and prone to bouts of neuroticism. Thanks to his membership at St. Thomas's, he avoided her as much as possible.

"Please excuse me for a moment, dear. I need to stretch my legs. My gout is playing up."

"Of course, my love."

O'Shea shuffled off down the ballroom towards a recessed connecting door. There stood Eliza in her dark evening dress, as well-camouflaged as a chameleon.

"Why aren't you in the slums where you belong? You had better leave quietly, or something unfortunate may happen to you."

"Don't cause a scene, Dennis."

Lord O'Shea was furious that she would fob him off.

"Why did you have to accept the invitation? I will haul Lord McGill over the coals for this mistake."

Dennis O'Shea grabbed her roughly and pulled her into a small service cupboard.

"I have missed you, Lizelle," he sneered, stroking her cheek, face just inches away from hers.

"Get off!"

"Shall I teach you a lesson for embarrassing me?"

They began to wrestle. Eliza shoved and kicked at him, desperate to get away.

"Eliza, Eliza. Where are you? I've got that drink you asked for."

It was Joey's voice, and she didn't want him to see her suffering. She'd have to be brave.

Dennis grabbed Eliza and cupped his hand over her mouth.

"Don't answer if you know what's good for you," he warned.

Joey's nose for trouble was twitching. Eliza would never wander off and leave him alone. He saw Ella moping alone and wondered what had happened to Dennis. He spotted a small chink of light leaking from under the service room door. He charged in and saw O'Shea accosting her. It was like a switch flicked in his brain. All he wanted to do was rescue the woman he regarded as the only mother he'd ever had—whatever the personal cost.

He saw a heavy-cut crystal vase and threw it at O'Shea's head. The vase hit Dennis on the temple, causing a great gash. The brute grabbed his handkerchief and held it to his temple.

"You little monster!"

"Leave him alone," said Eliza quietly. "If you touch him, I will get all my new friends in Spitalfields to ruin you."

Dennis fled. He would never antagonise Joey again, and he would never accost Eliza. He would simply go about his business as if they didn't exist.

*

Shaken by her encounter with Dennis, Eliza's appetite for socialising promptly left.

"Come on, Joey, let's go home. It has been a long night."

"I don't like it here, Eliza. I don't want to be rich. Nobody laughs or smiles. Nobody is friendly."

"You really do have a wise head on your shoulders, Master Cornish."

He grinned as he opened the door for her.

"Your uncle has spoken to me. How would you like to go and live in the country? We can live in a tiny village where everybody is friendly?"

"What about the business, Eliza? How will we survive?"

"Raffi says we have money to tide us over for many years, and we can always get the train to Spitalfields to work the market stall at the weekend if we wanted."

"What if that horrid Dennis follows us?"

"You have proven to be skilled with throwing vases, young man. I am sure you could throw a pitchfork at him or something?"

Joey doubled with laughter.

"I got him a good style, didn't I?"

"Yes, he won't bother us again."

"I'm glad you're not sending me to live with Mr Lawrence."

"You will always live with me, Joey. I'll never let you go. Clarice said she will visit soon to check how you're settling in."

"Will Jack visit too, Eliza?"

"I think Clarice will have something to say if
he doesn't."

Joey started to laugh.

"He really likes her, doesn't he?"

Eliza ignored the question.

"Want to head home, Joey?"

He nodded.

"How about we have a nice hot potato with
butter when we get back. I reckon they're
much nicer than those little vol-au-vents of
Lady McGill's."

"Yes. I've eaten a dozen, and I'm still starving.
Let's go!"

*

Eliza and Joey stood on the steps waiting for their cab.
The boy pulled his battered top hat down to keep his
ears warm. A lanky, hunched figure descended the steps
behind them.

"It can't be, can it? Lizelle?"

"Mr Featherstone! Fancy meeting you here.
And it's Eliza now. Part of the terms of the
divorce."

In the days of her marriage to Lord Dennis, Lizelle O'Shea had been a patron of the British Museum. He'd always liked her. She was kind and had never lauded her station over him. She was such a refreshing change to her ill-mannered husband.

Malcolm glanced at Joey. He'd been furious that the little terror had hidden in the museum and kicked him on the shin. His only redeeming factor was uncovering Abercrombie and Raubach's plot to swindle the museum.

"Thank you for enlightening us to the theft of the tablet," Mr Featherstone said to Joey stiffly.

"It is a pleasure, sir. Have they found it yet?"

"No."

Joey frowned.

"Am I allowed back in the museum?"

"Certainly. I will show you things you didn't see while you were there."

Joey nodded, still scared of Mr Featherstone.

The custodian drew Eliza aside.

"I have made many mistakes in my life. I need to make friends. I sacrificed my family for a building with old things in it. May I have the pleasure of taking you to tea? Perhaps the Lyon's Tea Shop on the Strand? I am told it's excellent."

"It will be my pleasure, Malcolm."

Mr Featherstone felt his spirits lift for the first time in years. He knew that all his recent woes were leading him towards a new life with new friends and new joy. He just hoped that Joey didn't prove to be a little pest if he tried to pursue Mrs O'Shea.

*

Jack and Clarice sneaked out of the party. They'd had their fill of enforced formality.

"Shall we get a cab, Clarry?"

"I quite fancy a stroll. Come on, it's not far back to our hotels."

They took a route that weaved its way through Grosvenor Square. The majestic white buildings encircled a small green, planted with beautiful shrubs and trees.

Suddenly, Clarice found herself following Jack towards a bench.

"Let's look up at the stars, shall we?"

"In this smog? What are you up to, Professor Wyatt?"

"Alright. You've sussed me. I wanted to be alone with you. You are so beautiful to me. Inside and out."

Clarice smiled.

Jack gently drew her into his arms, and they kissed. It was the single most wonderful moment of Clarice's life.

"We should be alone more often," Clarice confessed. "I rather like it."

"There's something else, Clarry. I need to tell you something. Something important. There will never be the right time or place to say this."

The words hit as hard as a punch. Soon she was absorbed in her own thoughts. Millions of them tumbled through her mind at the rate of knots. She knew what it was. The moment she had been dreading. The time to say goodbye. Attending the ball, this moment in the park, the first kiss was all a long, bittersweet goodbye. Why did she have to kiss him? Didn't she realise it would make parting more painful? At least she'd learned something about herself. She knew what type of man she wanted. She just couldn't have this one.

"Did you hear me?" Jack held her by the shoulders and looked down at her.

"Yes, it's time to say goodbye."

"Do I have to repeat everything I just said?"

"No, I heard it all," she lied, giving a nervous smile.

"Then say yes."

"Why?" Clarice frowned.

"I've just told you that I love you. I want to marry you."

Jack laughed and cradled her face in his hands.

"Do I have to do this to convince you?"

"Do what?"

The second kiss was better and longer than the first. When they surfaced for air, Clarice replied:

"Of course, I'll marry you!"

He took her hand and kissed the back of it. Suddenly, there was a loud snap and a flash.

"What was that?" whispered Clarice.

Jack jumped to his feet and saw a photographer scarpering off.

That picture would have made the society columns if Ambassador O'Rourke had not used his diplomatic skills to keep the saucy material out of the newspaper. Why did Wyatt always draw controversy? At least after meeting this Lawrence girl, he'd stopped getting drunk in the East End.

It wasn't long before Kyle heard that they were courting and had announced that they would marry within a month. The two-week engagement impressed O'Rourke—it was unusual for Jack Wyatt to show such restraint. He couldn't wait for Jack and Clarice to leave London and for his life to return to normal. Jack's whirlwind visit with the stone had been set at gale force for its entire duration, and poor O'Rourke felt he needed a month in the Swiss Alps to recuperate from it.

24

FACING THE CLIMB

The island was dry and rocky. It was covered in scrub. Goats and sheep grazed on whatever they could find between the white rocks that littered the landscape. The villages were old, as if stepping back hundreds of years. The sunshine baked on the cottage, and most of the day was spent sitting under a tree outside. Many visitors came and went, making daily bicycle trips to the picturesque market. The skies were bright blue, with not a hint of smog. The water was clean and clear.

Violet and Emilio sat overlooking the harbour. It was awash with loud, colourful activity, reflecting the very soul of Sicily.

They saw the fish spill from the fishing boat nets onto the wharves. They watched the crew struggle to shift a hefty crate onto a cart. The couple could see the surefooted donkey progressing up the hill with its precious cargo heading towards their little herder's cottage.

"I told you I would give you a new life," Emilio said.

From the moment he'd set foot on the sun-drenched island, Violet had seen the difference in him. He was relaxed, he laughed, and his family were joyful. This was where he belonged. Where they belonged.

"I didn't believe you. I didn't think you would want somebody like me, Emilio."

"We do what we need to survive, my love. But now it's time for us both to stop surviving and start living."

Emilio leaned over and kissed her.

She, too, had changed. She'd lost her pale, sickly pallor; she no longer lived in fear. She'd gained weight and soaked up the life and light around her.

"What are we going to do with that old rock?" she asked.

"It will go to Rome. The Vatican is prepared to reward us for it. It will live in the bowels of the great city forever. Nobody will lay eyes on it. It is another treasure for the church. We will have absolution forever."

Violet smiled up at him.

"Tell me about the future, Emilio."

He put his arm around her.

"Do you see that piece of land? I will buy it, and we will have our own farm. I will build you a house. It will have so many rooms, and we will have children."

Violet had heard his plans many times before, but this time, the dream was even closer as the donkey cart made itself up the steep hill. Emilio was fulfilling the promise.

————

Like The Forgotten Sister? Here are some more books in my 'Victorian Sisters Sagas' series you'll love. Have you read them all?

- mybook.to/VictorianSisterSagas

The Sailor's Lost Daughters

1870s Manchester. Twin girls are born to a struggling, sickly mother in the notorious Angel Meadow slum. With an absent father, when one girl gets separated from her family, can she survive alone?

The neglected daughters are cared for by an aunt who lacks any nurturing instincts. Soon, the siblings learn first-hand how difficult life can be in Victorian Manchester. Only the aunt's selfish desire to replace their mother in their father's heart keeps them alive. When Ruby and her aunt are separated at the market, only her twin sister cares about the girl's whereabouts.

Agnes hopes Ruby will die alone, leaving one less mouth to feed. As her relentless aunt pursues her self-interested goal, will the poor young girl ever see her devoted sister and loving sailor father again?

- viewbook.at/EHSailor

The Slum Sisters' Wish

Manchester 1880s: Two sisters struggle to make a new life in Salford despite the horrors of the slums. Each takes a different path to freedom. Despite the odds, can either succeed?

Trapped in a vicious cycle of poverty with a drunken mother and a sailor father always at sea, the girls risk everything to escape their miserable home. A desperate sister's careless act shatters the family's fragile unity. Everything they cling to is torn away. Only a perilous path forward remains. Will the rival sisters collapse under the strain and slump into oblivion in the notorious Angel Meadow? Or will their persistence lead them to freedom and true love?

- mybook.to/SlumSistersBL

GET THREE FREE AND EXCLUSIVE EMMA HARDWICK OFFERS

Hi! Emma here. For me, the most rewarding thing about writing books is building a relationship with my readers, and it's a true pleasure to share my experiences with you. From time to time, I write little newsletters with short snippets I discover as I research my Victorian historical romances, details that don't make it into my books. In addition, I also talk about how writing my next release is progressing, plus news about special reader offers and competitions.

And I'll include all these freebies if you join my newsletter:

- A copy of my introductory novella, The Pit Lad's Mother.

- A copy of my introductory short story, The Photographer's Girl.

- A free copy of my Victorian curiosities, a collection of newspaper snippets I have collated over the years that have inspired many of the scenes in my books.

These are all exclusive to my newsletter—you can't get them anywhere else. You can grab your free books on BookFunnel, by signing up here:

- https://rebrand.ly/eh-free

ENJOYED THIS BOOK? YOU CAN MAKE A BIG DIFFERENCE

Reviews are the most powerful tools in my arsenal when it comes to getting attention for my books. Much as I'd like to, I don't have the financial muscle of a New York publisher. I can't take out full-page ads in the newspaper, put posters on the subway, or appear on a prime-time chat show.

(Not yet, anyway).

But I do have something much more powerful and effective than that, and it's something that those publishers would kill to get their hands on—avid readers who are loyal and supportive.

Honest ratings and reviews of my books help bring them to the attention of others who will enjoy them. If you've got something to share about this book, I would be very grateful if you could spend just a minute or two leaving a review (it can be as short as you like) on the book's Amazon page.

If you're reading on Kindle, you can jump right to the review page by clicking the link below.

UK — US — AU — CA — DE — ES — FR — IT

I really appreciate your feedback. It helps me improve my books.

If you'd like to be a member of my 'Book Squad' and be an advance reviewer of my books before they are launched, you can find out more on the next page.

Here's my author page on Amazon for paperback readers.

CAN YOU HELP ME WITH MY NEXT BOOK?

Like the chance to read my stuff before it hits Amazon? Read on.

One of the best things I did last year was set up Emma's 'Book Squad'. Getting reviews on new books as soon as they launch is critically important. You probably weigh reviews highly when deciding whether to try a new author or rely on an old favourite—I know that I do. Apart from helping to persuade people to give a new writer a shot, reviews help drive early sales, which, in turn, means that Amazon takes notice and starts to tell more people about my books so more people can enjoy them.

To make that happen, I have a small team of 'advance readers'. It's pretty simple and is, I hope, good fun. It involves them being sent a copy of whatever book I've just finished and then, when it is published, firing up a quick and honest review. Simple as that. Some team members have picked up errors that I've been able to correct, and others have suggested changes to the plot that I have incorporated.

Besides getting a copy of the latest book before anyone else, I try to say thanks with some exclusive competitions. In some circumstances, I offer signed print editions, else things like limited edition mugs. I try to keep the team relatively compact. There are a couple of vacancies at the moment, and if you would like to get involved, please let me know. As an avid reader of my books, I'd love to receive your feedback.

You can apply here:

- https://bit.ly/EH-ST

ABOUT THE AUTHOR

Emma Hardwick is the author of several series of Victorian historical saga romances. She lives in London with her husband and dogs and makes her online home at:

- www.emmahardwick.co.uk

You can connect with Emma on Facebook at :
- www.facebook.com/emmahardwickauthor

and if the mood takes you, you should send her an email at:

- hello@emmahardwick.co.uk

ALSO BY EMMA HARDWICK

Here's a complete set of all my historical romance series. You can view all my books on my Amazon author page.

The Hudson Family Saga

Set in Victorian England, two heartrending tales of torment, struggle, and love that follow the Hudsons between 1849 up to the late 1890s. Join the heroines, determined to fight for their own independence and success, no matter what grave betrayals, hardships, and catastrophes befall them.

See all books in the series

- https://rebrand.ly/HFSaga

The Victorian Runaway Girls

Join these tenacious Victorian women as they strive to break from their bleak past and bring true love into their future. Whether abandoned, forgotten, or mistreated, each of the women has a reason to flee and never return.

See all books in the series

- https://rebrand.ly/RGSaga

The Victorian Christmas Chronicles

Get into the festive spirit and join these vivacious, strong Victorian lasses fighting for a brighter future, despite many cruel obstacles in these feel-good tales of courage and determination, each with a wonderful yuletide backdrop.

See all books in the series

- https://rebrand.ly/CCSaga

Printed in Great Britain
by Amazon